THE AIRSHIP

INCANTATIONS

THE AIRSHIP

INCANTATIONS

ADAM TIPPS WEINSTEIN

FC2
TUSCALOOSA

FC2 is an imprint of The University of Alabama Press

Inquiries about reproducing material from this work should be addressed to the University of Alabama Press

Book Design: Publications Unit, Department of English, Illinois State
    University; Director: Steve Halle, Production Intern: Katelyn Kern,
    Production Assistant: Bryanna Tidmarsh
Cover Design: Lou Robinson
Typeface: Baskerville

Library of Congress Cataloging-in-Publication Data is available from the
Library of Congress.

ISBN: 978-1-57366-187-4
E-ISBN: 978-1-57366-889-7

–FOR Z & E–

With Love and Gratitude

CONTENTS

A lived event is finite, concluded at least on the level of experience. But a remembered event is infinite, a possible key to everything that preceded it and to everything that will follow.

ἀλλ’ ἄγε μοι τόδε εἰπὲ καὶ ἀτρεκέως κατάλεξον
But come tell me this, and recount it exactly

This is not a book. This is spiritualism.

PROLOGUE

THEY CALLED HIM "THE WANDERING JEW." They called him "The Man Without a Country." Newspapers that carried Nathan Cohen's story featured a grainy mugshot of a gaunt man in a black wool jacket, with a heavy beard and heavy black eyes, staring from the railing of a huge passenger steamship, the *Vasari*, on which he had been sailing non-stop for the last year.

Nathan Cohen had been deported from the United States as a derelict and a madman in 1912 and was ordered to be returned to his port of origin. In his personal effects was a ticket on the passenger steamship *Vasari*, travelling from Buenos Aires, 1910, so that is where he was remitted. From New York he sailed to Argentina; having no official documents or papers, he was rejected. He returned to the ship and went north again, and again, at Ellis Island, he was denied entry. Around and around he went, country-less and stateless.

Nathan Cohen, they said, was destined to spend the rest of his life on the high seas.

As things went, Cohen's case wasn't unusual. There were steady streams of emigrants fleeing wars, conquests, and colonialism the world over—the Franco-Prussian War, the Austro-Prussian War, the Serbian-Ottoman Wars, the Russo-Turkish War, the Japanese invasion of Taiwan, the Boxer Rebellion, the Mexican Revolution. Landgrabs for territory in Africa were so widespread and impassioned that German Chancellor Otto von Bismarck convened the Berlin Conference (Kongokonferenz) in 1884 to establish rules and etiquettes for usurping and annexing African territories. Passenger-shipping veins were clotted and atrophied with the recently dispossessed.

In many ways, the captain of the *Vasari*, James Cadogan, had it easy. Nathan Cohen spoke little and dressed inappropriately, but in the six months Cohen had been aboard the ship, his only habit seemed to be sweeping the length of the deck, day in and day out. Though grizzled and gnarled like an old root, he was unexceptional and harmless. Cadogan decided it was best to let Nathan Cohen recover from his illness in whatever way served him best.

Between 1912 and 1914, Nathan Cohen made the round trip ten times, New York to Argentina and then back again. And then one night, toward the end of May, only weeks before what was later called the "Guns of August," when German troops broke treaty and marched through neutral Belgium on their way to invading France, and as the moon rose high in the western sky, a handful of late-night revelers who were gathered on one of the upper observation decks of the *Vasari* saw a strange little aircraft conjured from the fog at the bow.

The lower part of the airship was a square wooden raft, and it rose through the air attached to a magnificently colored balloon. There was a square hole cut through the bottom of the raft, out of which poked an obscure little outboard engine that whirred and spat and farted black clouds of smoke, as it turned a propeller. Aboard the raft was a coal brazier and a bellows, which exhaled hot air into an opening on the underside of the balloon.

Seated at the rear of the raft like a small captain was the little dog, Laika, who had gone missing only a month or two before. Later, one of the deck hands who also saw the airship confirmed the dog as the same one that had belonged to the opera singer Salomé Amvrosiivka Krushelnytska, and whose shaggy-bearded muzzle had more recently been seen around the black-haired Jew who tended to the horses.

The airship swayed and creaked as it sailed above their heads. It strained against its hempen ropes. The dog barked at them once, twice, and then the apparition passed over the gunwales, the capstan, and then beyond. It headed west towards the open water, rising and sailing towards the moon as if caught in the tug of light. Soon the raft was only a vanishing black dot, and then it was swallowed into the face of the moon and it was gone.

Later, they found that Nathan Cohen also had gone missing. Folded neatly atop the straw of his bed in the hayloft were a of pair socks, a wool blanket, and a note, "THANK YOU," written in block letters. In the crease of the note was Cohen's original ticket, dated from October of 1910: *Vasari*. Destination: New York. 80 reals. On the reverse side of the ticket was a sketchy map that traced a path through the stars.

ONE

A FABLE

AFTER THE ENSLAVED ISRAELITES FLED EGYPT, they sent twelve spies into the desert to scout the territories that were promised to them by God. Ten of the twelve spies gave unpleasant reports about the new lands, and this angered God. As punishment, they were made to wander in the desert for forty years so that only their children would enter the "land flowing with milk and honey."

In their diaspora, God was with the Israelites in the form of the eternal flame, the *ner tamid*. The lamp burned inside the tabernacle, the provisional sanctuary the Jewish peoples carried with them through the eternal deserts. They called the light *Shekhinah*, the "dwelling place" of HaShem in exile.

During Sukkot, the Feast of Tabernacles, we remember the diaspora by building *sukkah* ("booths") in the fields. The huts are made from the "branches of palm trees, and boughs of leafy trees, and willows of the brook." These are temporary shelters, and we camp for seven days and seven nights in the *sukkah* so that "All who are native Israelites may know that I made the children of Israel dwell in booths when I brought them out of the land of Egypt."

In the apocrypha of the *Sefer Yetzirah*—the ancient, Jewish mystical text of the *Zohar*, "The Book of Formation"— *Shekhinah* is the liminal space between the trunk and the roots of the Tree of Life. "In the Beginning, writes the great Kabbalist magician Reb Eliyahu Ba'al Shem, *Ein Sof*, the Infinite One, was everywhere. The Holy Spirit made a space for creation by drawing in a deep breath. The clearing is sometimes called the Divine Exile, and into that hollow Creation burst like a flood. Perfection was forever shattered, and the river of genesis bifurcated and branched. The splinters of Divinity became the ten *sefirot*, which are sometimes called the *shemot* ("names"), *orot* ("lights"), *neti'ot* ("shoots"), *mekorot* ("sources"), or *ketarim* ("crowns") of the Divine, and as the ten branches of the Tree of Life.

The energy flows from *Keter*, the crown at the top, the incomprehensible and the beyond, down to the root-*sefirot*, *Malkuth*, the earth realm. "Malkuth receives the effulgence of other sefirot yet none flows from it," the Ba'al Shem writes. "Malkuth has nothing of its own. The light emanated from it is reflected light, like that of the moon." This is why *Shekhinah* is called the spirit of dwelling. Divinity is manifest in the very soil from which the bodies of our progenitors were formed; upon our deaths, the energy is returned in the offering of our decay. According to the Kabbalists, when *Malkuth* achieves eminent stillness, the reflection of the light it bears upon its surface is untampered with, and therefore it is perfect, "like a transparent eyeball." Below *Malkuth* are the domains of the *lilit*, the wanton temptresses of the night, where "Wildcats shall meet with hyenas," and "goat-demons shall call to each other." "There too Lilith shall repose," we read in Isaiah, "and find a place to rest."

The *sukkah* is called the "shadow of faith" because in the *sukkah* hut we are unprotected, except by the love of God. During the seven nights of Sukkot we make our beds on the ground. The walls of the hut are made from *galam*, "reeds." "Neither bush or tree," *galam* signifies the temporariness of the shelter. The roof, too, must not be fully covered so that the stars will be visible through its cracks. We stare up through the imperfect thatch and recall a faith knitted to impermanence in exile, and we invite the spirit of *Shekinah* to rest with us. We notice that there are many entrances and exits to the *sukkah*. Almost like a burrow, the hut is more landscape than dwelling. The hut is a thousand plateaus. It claims no territory of its own. And nowhere else but in *sukkah* do we sleep this close to death, or to the source of all life.

TWO

SOME EVENTS CONCERNING THE YEAR 1912—THE TAROT OF THE SHIP—DISCOVERIES IN THE CARGO HOLD—DREAMS OF THE PAST

SEPTEMBER, 1912. The launch of the airship was a year and a half away. Hurricane-force storms rolled across the Atlantic. They spun up from the great basin and swept west across the Dominican Republic, Haiti, and Cuba, making landfall north and south in the Gulf. From the safety of the ship, the passengers on the Vasari gathered to watch black thunderclouds cross the horizon. When the winds changed direction, they stiffened if they felt the breeze turn to face them. The superstitious spat.

In Mexico, the monsoon rains arrived just as the suspicious death of Major Francisco Cárdenas was reported in local newspapers. Cárdenas was a member of the *rurales*, the government forces in Mexico City, who were doing battle against the nationalist rebel forces. Cárdenas commanded the escort for the deposed president and vice president to prison—Francisco Madero and Pino Suárez respectively—when the party undertook fire from bandits and the overthrown leaders were killed.

Deposed President Madero had failed at his project of a constitutional democracy, having run up against irreconcilable differences with the various political factions in Mexico—most famously the Zapatistas in Chihuahua, who fought for land reform against the corporate consolidation of their ancestral farms by the *dueños* of the Terrazas monopoly, and for whom the famous Pancho Villa, née José Doroteo Arango Arámbula, commanded the *División del Norte*. But Madero could not have predicted how far Manuel Mondragón, a relatively unknown officer in the capital city, and also a leader in the *rurales*, would go to cover up crimes of embezzlement and corruption. Although the overthrow of Madero was only weakly supported in the capital city, Mondragón and a few cadets took the coup d'etat upon themselves, installing Victoriano Huerta in Madero's stead. Thus, it came to be that, on their way to prison, the overthrown president and vice president were murdered, and it had been generally understood that the cheating scoundrel Cárdenas himself put the rifle to Madero's head. In fact, he is said to have boasted of it.

Enemies predicted Cárdenas' life would be a short one, and that at the first favorable opportunity he would *be removed* in order to eliminate the possibility of his ever telling the truth of the assassination, or under whose orders it was performed. The newspaper reports of his death, therefore, must have proven satisfactory to such revenge-minded parties.

In Vienna, the Austrian Emperor Franz Josef gave a speech that "aroused general anxiety and considerable excitement." By the end of 1912, Serbia had conquered most of Albania in the First Balkan War and was expanding south towards the Adriatic Sea. Fearing the rise of Serbian power and Serbia's alignment with Russia, Austria's sworn enemy, Austria strove to block Serbia's access to the Adriatic. Austria sought peaceful arbitration with the leaders of Europe at the Conference in London claiming their interference in the region was justified by Serbian atrocities committed against the Albanians: "On the march through Albania to the sea the Servians did not only treacherously murder and execute armed Albanians, but their beast-like cruelty did not stop at falling upon unarmed and defenseless persons, old men and women, children and infants at the breast," the Austrians reported.

In Franz Joseph's speech, however, authorities noted "the great reserve in the Austrian Emperor's address and the omission of all reference to future peace," and they regarded the passage in which he intimated that Austria-Hungary must be prepared for eventualities on land and sea "as especially ominous."

In Latvia, the news from Ukraine and Odessa, and from St. Petersburg and Warsaw murmured disaster—pogroms against the Jews, fires, beatings, murder.

* * *

The first few months after Cohen had been deported, he kept to himself, only venturing out in the evenings to take meals with the other third-class passengers. As one voyage crossed into the next, and then the next after that, he watched the ship's goings-on play out as a Tarot of limited possibility, reshuffled and dealt again as the passengers boarded and debarked. There were bulletins throughout the ship that advertised the various timetables—mealtimes, cabin checks, the daily raising and lowering of the flag, cocktail hours, etc. and according to which the ship's doings could, at any moment, be foretold. The precision with which these events actually unfolded according to those orders might have been astonishing if it weren't for the high standards of the Lamport & Holt Co.

On the first day there were the greetings and welcomes. There was an opening night gala for first-class passengers featuring a service of *Hors d'Œuvres Varies*, *Consommé Orientale*, *Frit Tartare*, *Filet de Bœuf*, *Jardinere Braisé*, *Chapon Roti au Jambon*, *Salade de fruits*, *Pudding Diplomate*, and *Glace Fédor*. There was dancing and music on the upper and middle decks, with big bands playing "The Trail of the Lonesome Pine," "Gasoline," "Ballin' the Jack," and "El Cóndor Pasa" one year; "The Aba Daba Honeymoon," "Keep the Home Fires Burning," "Your King and Country Want You," and "I Want to Go Back to Michigan," the next.

Over the next week the guests settled into daily routines of strolling and group exercise, bull-board, quoit, shuffleboard, tea and novels, and quiet conversations in various salons. Guests were recommended to take in "the breath of the sea, with its health-giving ozone; new vistas from day to day; the psychological stimulus of new environments and new acquaintances; and all the experiences which render an ocean voyage on such a ship a treasure-house of pleasant memories."

Twelve days after leaving New York they arrived at Barbados, which the *Vasari*'s brochure described as "Sugar plantations, windmills, and picturesque native life." A fine lunch was served at the Marine Hotel.

They sailed around the horn of Brazil and docked in Bahia, where guests debarked for day tours in the "idyllic city surrounded by coastal waters, with warehouses and factories built very much in colonial fashion: large, colorful square buildings with gabled rooftops."

In Santos, they discovered "the most important coffee port of Brazil, and one of the oldest European settlements. In common with St. Paulo, it owed its origin to the first shipwreck on the island of St. Vincente."

Montevideo was the "cultured capital of Uruguay."

And Rio de Janeiro, capital of Brazil, "was one of the world's handsomest cities. The unrivalled bay flanked by mountains, dotted with islands, and encircled by a splendid esplanade, park and boulevard...The Avenida Central, Avenida do Mangue, and Avenida Jardin, famous for their beauty." Passengers made excursions by rail to Corcovado, the mountain resorts of Tijuca, Santa Theresa, and Sumaré; and by ferry and rail to fashionable and charming Petropolis, nestled in a basin in the Serra da Estrela.

Although nowhere near the size of the largest of the passenger ships—twin-propeller behemoths like the *Lusitania* (31,550 Gross Tons), the *Mauretania* (31,938 GT), the *Olympic* (45,324 GT), and the *Titanic* (46,328 GT)—the *Vasari*, weighing in at 10,117 Gross Tons, accommodated nearly six hundred passengers: one hundred in first-class, two hundred in second-class, and three hundred in third-class. "A good ship is a good home," said the brochure. "It is more than that. It comprises the range of conveniences that characterize modern hotels of the first class. The amplest provision is made for the comfort of pleasure tourists, while capacious carrying capacity admits of larger commercial cargos, which at the same time add to the steadiness of the vessel."

At each port, Cohen stayed aboard the ship. He spoke to no one. Time idled forward, then it reversed—going and then coming back. He marked the passing seasons by the waning colors along the wooded coasts in the north, the fierce storms that followed the tides of the Gulf Stream, and the shape and curl of a wave on a cloudless October day, with no land in sight, and the water aping the color of sky.

After six months, the crew began to offer Cohen odd jobs. They took pity on him. It was as if he had become their albatross. Like the Ancient Mariner, Cohen was doomed to wander forever; as the sailors' own fates were knitted to his, he stitched a bond for safe passage. As long as he was sheltered in their drift, so would they sail unharmed by any of the dangers that lurked in the Atlantic—this in the midst of global political uncertainty. Across the ocean, Serbian operatives from the Black Hand had engaged, and it was only a matter of time before Archduke Ferdinand would be assassinated by the anarchist Gavrilo Princip, in Sarajevo, as the Archduke's motorcade came around an unprotected corner, and days later Europe would be plunged into war. With Cohen aboard, the *Vasari* might continue its lemniscate crossings of the Atlantic, as if the rest of the world were only a rumor.

One day a passing cabin boy handed Cohen a broom, and like a wooden top, Cohen was set into motion. Day in and day out he swept.

In the mornings Cohen began on one side of the ship, sweeping along the narrow corridors and back stairs, and any other out-of-the-way place. On the port side were the first-class salons, the billiard rooms, smoking rooms, and libraries. Cohen always arrived below the ballroom in the late morning—the sun on the port side as they journeyed towards South America, and starboard coming back—when the orchestra was practicing. The jumble of noise filled the steel-paneled fire tunnels like a haunting. Sometimes it was almost deafening in its intensity; other times a timid violin was like a mouse hiding somewhere just beyond in the periphery of the shadows.

Afternoons, Cohen found himself at the fore observation deck, where, on a clear, bright blue day, there was little except the wind and the unfolding infinity before him. Gulls hovered there in the opposing air currents, like the taxidermied birds that hang from the ceilings of the various natural history museums the world over. Only, if you watched the gulls carefully, they would steadily rise higher into the cobalt skies and then settle gently back towards the earth again, away and then back, away and then back like breathing.

Then Cohen turned around, beginning his reverse through the bowels of the ship. He crossed the catwalk in the main cargo hold, and through the dark of the centerline. Above hung the long necks of the loading cranes that kept vigil over the towers of crates and boxes. He descended the corkscrew stairs to the fire tunnels that ran the *Vasari*'s lateral lines. The industrial passageways were a convenient way for a ghost to pass from one part of the ship to another. Under the galleys were the crew's berths, a honeycomb of light that glowed like a reliquary.

Passing further down, Cohen's lantern light showed the bolted lines of the steel panels of the hull, like the suture marks on a skull. There were intermittent, terrifying bursts of *whip-crack!*, the pistol shots of a god. If you weren't prepared for it—the ripping sound created by the steel hulk aligning itself with the impossible pressure of displaced water—you'd swear the hull had burst along those lines and in a moment would be the barreling rush and collapse of the sea.

The stitches revealed where the hull was given permission to breathe, where it contracted, where it dilated. Dead things like the ship could hold their breath, but only if they were allowed to bend and wince as they dived into the deep. New experimental German U-boats, for example, could plunge to one hundred forty fathoms. Even then, the crews of those boats were known to go further to avoid detection. Then the lungs began to collapse and the seams unravel. Rise, pump the water from the lungs, repair the busted seams. "Of all divers," says the poet—"thou hast dived the deepest. That head upon which the upper sun now gleams, has moved amid this world's foundations." "Speak mighty head, and tell us the secret thing that is in thee." But the ships that reach the bottom are silent.

In the *Vasari*'s cargo holds, Cohen was presented with riddles. Once, in the deepest parts of the maze of closets, storerooms, and linking passageways, he found thirty-four matching red crates containing the cast replica of *Diplodocus carnegii*, "Dippy," who was being transported from the Carnegie Museum in New York to Buenos Aires. For thirty years, casts had been sent all over the world: to the Royal Museum in Berlin, the Natural History Museum in Paris, the Imperial Museum in Vienna, and the Imperial Academy of Science in St. Petersburg, Russia, among others. The one caveat was that the gift of a *Diplodocus* could only be requested through an official plea by the president of the country in question. Thus, when an Argentinian ambassador applied for a cast, he was rejected. However, when the Argentinean president, Dr. Roque Sáenz Peña, made a formal appeal, his application was accepted.

And so it was that "Dippy," the cast skeleton of an extinct dinosaur, weighing ten thousand pounds, measuring eighty-four feet long, and whose Adamic model had been excavated in eastern Wyoming, was on its way to the Museo de La Plata. The neatly labeled plaster bones were buried in straw and sealed in huge wooden crates that were nailed shut and stacked in orderly rows in an out-of-the-way spot below the water-line of the great Atlantic steamship, and accompanied by Dr. William Holland and Mr. Arthur Coggeshall of the Carnegie Museum, who smoked cigars and dined upstairs.

After the cargo holds was the buried warm heart of the ship, the galley kitchens, where huge, coal-fired ovens made short work of the various breads, rolls, baguettes, loaves, scones, and boules that fed upwards of seven hundred passengers and crew a day. Past the bakery was the main kitchen, where another line of ovens was driven by steam that was piped directly from the ship's main boiler, and which were pressure-sealed behind gigantic steel wheels. When the pressure was released the room was filled with clouds of steam. Suddenly a cook carrying a tray of vivid orange carrots, or green stems of broccoli, or a silver platter of the whitest, flakiest, delicate white sole, each filet bedecked with a yellow lemon slice and finished with a sprig of curly green parsley, emerged from the fog.

Below the galleys was the vegetable and grain hold, and it was here, amongst the must of fresh things clasping to life, that Cohen found a quiet seat and table in two overturned crates. He removed his hat and pulled at his beard. He scratched one leg, then the other. He snuffed the lamp and was alone in the dark of the cold-storage, where the smell of humus and soil still clung to crates of vegetables, and to the russet sacks of potatoes. Dozing in the quiet of the belly of the ship, he followed a cunicular memory into the dreamy present of a late fall day in Bauska.

Breathe. It was the *zelta rudens*, the golden days of autumn. Cohen and his father drove the plow along the river Drina, alongside chugging watermills and creeping coal barges. Cohen tripped and leapt before the plow, watching for debris, and keeping an eye on the texture of the soil.

His father sat atop the wagon singing in heavy, rhythmic Yiddish that folded into the sound of the plow tugging through the soil, the snorting of the horses, and the cries of birds behind them that dove for the bugs and worms and other things that were turned up. A single crow followed behind them, waiting for a meal to surface.

Beyond, in the fields, men and women in black wool and white linen swung scythes and rakes though the wheat disturbing clouds of insects that leapt skyward. The smell of cut grass and earth was everywhere.

In town, the people were equally busy with the harvest. Wagons loaded with produce rolled through the unpaved streets. Purveyors shouted the litanies of produce—Marants iz a mer, gel iz a barne, grin iz di zeneft!—to people who leaned from apartment windows, washed and hung laundry, and mended and painted walls; to children playing in front yards with hoops and string; and to those who spent their last summer days sitting idly in rocking chairs on their porches, with heavy woolen blankets, watching the life of the shtetl move abundantly onward.

Smell. The wagons trailed the scent of onions, carrots, spinach, mustard, field peas, and bush beans; the heavy molder of melons, just this side of death, so sweet when picked and eaten first thing in the morning, before the heat of the day set upon them.

See. There were six varieties of corn, others for flint, popcorn, and meal. There were late season tomatoes in deepest purples, ambers, and yellows, and paste tomatoes as red as blood. There were cartloads of potatoes like marching hills. Of all the produce, only the rye, wheat, barley, and apples were native to Bauska. Most of the other crops had come back with the *conquistadores* from the New World.

At home Cohen's mother set out rows of glass jars, steaming after a hot-water bath. They were filled with green tomatoes and cucumbers, and spiked with dill, heads of garlic, and whole paprika. She sealed the jars with wax, and set them in the cellar next to stores of beets, green beans, carrots, cabbage, peppers, and more. In another week they would bring home late-season berries, and she would make jam and preserves.

They would have bushels of apples and pears for cider. Outside, salted meat and fish dried in the sun.

September, October—Cohen and his father ranged all over the Pale. They plowed and harrowed, preparing the ground for next year's planting. Where the soil had been overworked—where it was too fine, too gray, odorless, tasteless—they broadcast clover, meal-rye, and black barley, which, when fully grown, would be cut down and turned back into the earth in the spring. The green manure would decay in the hot summer sun, and in the course of the season, the soil would be nourished back to life.

December, when the first hard snows came, and the tributaries and canals turned to veins of ice. Cords of split wood were piled as high as the roof. The hayloft was full. They made pots of plaster mixed with straw to patch the chinks in the walls where the wind had begun to whistle through. The thick gray of winter settled upon them like a low roof.

Decay: the smell of turned earth stitched together the dark of the *Vasari*'s green-hold to Cohen's childhood home in those ancient Baltic farmlands. Off the coast of New York, the ship sped through flurries of snow. Deep below, one fertile dark led into another, and Cohen wandered between those worlds for weeks, or months, or maybe years.

* * *

On March 28, 1913, one day before the *Vasari*'s return departure, and at the conclusion of Cohen's first year at sea, the magnificent *Teatro Colón* in beautiful downtown Buenos Aires, showed Wagner's *Lohengrin*, with Salomé Krushelnytska as Elsa, the doomed princess, and Pavel Ludikar as the Percivalean knight who vows to fight for her honor, so long as she never asks after his identity. Cohen, who had climbed to the promenade deck to see the lights of Buenos Aires, could not hear Krushelnytska perform, though it was her dog, Laika, who, through a series of coincidences and luck, would stand as pilot on the tiny airship when it sailed into the western sky on the morning of Wednesday, May 14, 1914, a year later.

On the day the *Vasari* departed, an article reported on the rumor of stolen mummies aboard a passenger steamer. "Trophies from Slain Bandits Turn Out To Be Parts of Mummies," the headline read. "Old Heads Start Tales on Ship." Apparently, there were rumors that "a bloodthirsty Americano" on a Lamport & Holt passenger line had brought aboard the heads of three Peruvian bandits who had held him up on his journey through a southern spur of the Andes. Soon after the vessel docked at Ellis Island, customs officials declared that they had looked carefully through all pieces of baggage, but had found no Peruvian heads. Finally, after much investigation, Dr. S. A. Davis, the ship's surgeon, laughed and admitted that it was he who had the mummified heads of two ancient Peruvian chiefs. He wasn't sure, however, how anyone had found out about them, or, more importantly, how the rumor had spread that they were the heads of slain bandits who had been surprised when their victim fought back. "Old heads start tales indeed," he said, with a twinkle in his eye.

Across the Gulf of Mexico, three masked robbers, part of the Martone gang, held up and robbed the New York—New Orleans express of the Alabama Great Southern railway in Tuscaloosa, escaping with $100,000. The gang fled in the locomotive of the train they robbed, exchanging shots with the posse which pursued them in a switch engine.

Meanwhile, Austria sent eighteen battalions to Bosnia and Herzegovina, which officials called "Dangerous but not hopeless."

A few weeks later, the *Vasari* crossed the equator, and passengers shed their wools and silks for bathing costumes and light tunics.

THREE

A BRIEF HISTORY OF BAUSKA AND THE RUSSIAN PALE OF SETTLEMENT—HOW NATHAN COHEN FIRST CAME TO ARGENTINA—DOWN THE RÍO DE LA PLATA—LAS PAMPAS—SUKKOT

NATHAN COHEN DEPARTED BAUSKA IN 1901. The town was part of the Russian-Jewish Pale of Settlement in the vast bogs, grasslands, and forests that fell between the eastern border of Germany and the western wall of Russia, not far from Moscow. The northern shoreline followed the brackish, ice age Baltic Sea. This was the Russian grain belt: a land of timber, iron, copper, tallow, hemp, flax, corn, wood, and wheat.

Bauska had once been part of the Duchy of Courland, which had once been part of the Kingdom of Poland, dissolved in the Third Partition of Poland in 1795. After the Second World War, the Baltic territories would eventually become Estonia, Lithuania, Latvia, and Poland. After Poland was taken by Princess Sophie of Anhalt-Zerbst, more commonly known as Catherine the Great, Empress of Russia, land in the duchy was granted to the Jews and others in order to hasten settlement of the newly acquired territories.

Since the inception of the Pale of Settlement, many of the Jewish *miasteczkos* and *shtetlekhs* had become famous for their industry and prosperity. There were the great towns of Dvinsk, Kurzeme, Zemgale, Vidzeme. There was Ludza, overshadowed by the twin spires of the Orthodox church, and the ruins of the

Livonian castle. Daugavpils, home of the great factories of the Jewish capitalists, with thirty-four synagogues, a hospital, a nursing home, and a theatre. Later, on June 26, 1941, in the dark days of the Second World War, 1,150 Daugavpils Jews would be shot dead by Nazis, and the rest transported to the camps.

After the assassination of Alexander II in 1881, and the false allegations of Jewish involvement, anti-Jewish riots were increasing. There was terror, and there was worse to come. In Kishinev, newspapers reported,

> riots were worse than the censor will permit to publish. There was a well laid-out plan for the general massacre of Jews on the day following the Orthodox Easter. The mob was led by priests, and the general cry, "Kill the Jews", was taken up all over the city. The Jews were taken wholly unaware and were slaughtered like sheep. The dead number 120 and the injured about 500. The scenes of horror attending this massacre are beyond description. Babies were literally torn to pieces by the frenzied and bloodthirsty mob. The local police made no attempt to check the reign of terror. At sunset the streets were piled with corpses and wounded. Those who could make their escape fled in terror.

As a result, the port cities were full of Jews who, like Cohen, boarded steamers for the United Kingdom, Hamburg, Hangau, Guberniya, and Helsinki, then onto North and South America, South Africa, or anywhere else.

Cohen sailed from Riga, on the northern coast of Latvia, around the horn of Denmark, to England; then south along the European coast down to Dakar, which juts out from the tip of Senegal, Africa like a finger pointing west. There he boarded in steerage on one of the titanic trans-Atlantic oceanliners, the *SS Halle*, and crossed to Brazil.

Cohen and seven hundred emigrants were caged in steerage in the lowest decks. There was hay on the floor for sleeping, and there were portable iron berths. They were so tightly packed there was no room to lie down. There was filth and shit in the corners and the heavy miasma of disease was visibly thick like springtime pollen. For exercise, they were allowed to promenade on the upper deck, the circuit of which was just over a mile. They were shipped from one port to the next, sometimes held in quarantine hostels for indefinite periods, then shuttled on towards whatever might follow.

Weeks passed, a dark press of time. And then came a sudden release. One day they arrived at port Río, the same shores the *conquistadores* had sailed to five hundred years before, and abruptly, for Cohen, the months of misery and wonder, and shock and anticipation; of being told to follow this line, to raise his arms and show the soles of his feet, and to spread out his belongings and to speak and to remain silent; of people and then more people, and tongues pining prayers culled from all directions of Europe and Russia; and of time elapsing, folding back on itself, slowing down, or disappearing all out of sorts— just like that, the voyage was over. Nathan Cohen had arrived. He was ready to begin his new life as a *gaucho* in las pampas.

The *SS Halle* docked in Bélem, in the great delta that forms the Baia de Marajó on the northeastern coast of Brazil, the largest drainage delta of the Amazon River Basin. When Charles Darwin moored there on his voyage on the Beagle, he reported "Delight itself, however, is a weak term to express the feelings of a naturalist who, for the first time, has wandered by himself in a Brazilian forest... The noise from the insects is so loud, that it may be heard even in a vessel anchored several hundred yards from the shore; yet within the recesses of the forest a universal silence appears to reign. To a person fond of natural history, such a day as this brings with it a deeper pleasure than he can ever hope to experience again."

Some fifty years later, the famous American naturalist John Muir said in an interview that "Man has done nothing as yet—comparatively speaking—with the river Amazon. In fact you might say that he is scarcely in evidence there at all. But the time will come," Muir continues, "when this whole region will be transformed into one of the richest garden spots of the earth, the seat of a civilization greater and more far-reaching than that found today in the Mississippi Valley...When that time comes the inexhaustible resources of the Amazon Valley will be discovered. When the rest of the garden spots of the earth are either worked out or overcrowded—posterity will have a place to thrive in and spread itself...and it will be possible for a native race to grow up full of vigor and the enterprise that accomplishes great things."

At Bélem, Cohen joined with twenty-two other "Russo" Jews bound for Moisésville, in the badlands of Santa Fe. In the 1870s, under the leadership of General Julio Argentino Roca, Argentina had begun the Conquista del Desierto, a plan to take Patagonia for the Argentinians. "Our self-respect," said

Roca, "as a virile people obliges us to put down as soon as possible, by reason or by force, this handful of savages who destroy our wealth and prevent us from definitively occupying, in the name of law, progress and our own security the richest and most fertile lands of the Republic." By 1890 his troops had killed over a thousand Indians, and displaced over fifteen thousand more. In all, the Conquista resulted in 86 million acres taken from the Indians. Among those who resettled *el desierto* were emigrant Jews who arrived in the badlands in 1898 and eventually founded the kibbutz at Moisésville.

From the mouth of the Madeira, Cohen and the other emigrants ferried to the Río de la Plata, where the waters were stained gold. Monsoon rains had washed away parts of the riverbanks, and the water was clogged with debris. They transferred to a steam-powered riverboat that belched smoke as it chugged upriver. Parrots, kites, and eagles fished overhead, and dolphin and loggerhead turtles skirted their boat.

At Itacoatiara, some of the passengers debarked to join the throngs John Muir had seen "rushing for fortunes, half crazy, half merry, daring fevers, debilitating heat, and dangers of every sort to pull rubber from the trees." This was central Brazil, and the heart of the rubber boom. "If one rubber baron bought a vast yacht, another would install a tame lion in his villa, and a third would water his horse on champagne."

Some of the passengers departed with picks and shovels at Minas-Geräes, to sink ambition into volcanic sands in search of diamonds.

At Porto Vehlo, more went to work on the Madeira-Mamoré, the Devil's Railroad, where the bodies of vast numbers of Indians disappeared to work deep below the surface of the earth in the diamond and gold mines, never to be seen again. Bodies were burned by the cartload. Smoke and ash drifted towards the river, settled on the water, and then vanished.

In Misiones, Cohen's ship entered a landscape of rolling green hills. It rained every day, and they huddled in the limited shelter of a canopy made of thatched banana leaves.

They were joined by a guide, Mr. Taylor, who spoke loudly and to no one in particular from his perch at the bow, where he sat beneath a heavily waxed canvas umbrella. He spoke of *la selva*, the jungles beyond, and of the savages who killed their enemies and preserved their heads as trophies. He had been offered a head, he said, for one hundred dollars in gold, the head as big as a fist. The bones had been removed, and the black skin was so carefully shrunken that none of the features were lost. He refused it, he said. He feared the ghost would haunt him for the rest of his life.

Further along Mr. Taylor pointed to a rope ladder on the banks of the river. The Jivaro, he said, they're polygamists, with eight or ten wives. They kill each other in feuds and sleep in a sitting posture with a spear between the knees. And they're superstitious. They have witch doctors who drink of *hiahuasa*, and it makes them see visions and dreams. He had drunk some, and spots came in front of his eyes. A little later he saw visions of saints.

Cohen and his companions transferred to another steamboat at Asunción, near Iguazu Falls, and continued south along the Paraná, which divides Brazil and Argentina. Alvar Nunez Cabeza de Vaca was the first Spanish explorer to arrive at the Paraná in 1561. In his diaries he describes the Iguaces, the peoples of the Paraná, as "killing their own children and buying those of strangers." Their principle food, he wrote, was "three kinds of roots, which they hunt for all over the land, and it takes two days to roast. They also eat spiders and ant eggs and worms and lizards and salamanders, and they drink potions made from the fangs of deadly vipers."

The land was low and marshy, a blanket of heat. Crossing into Argentina, the vegetation became sparse. The red river plateau seeped iron, and the river twisted through barren canyons while vultures circled overhead. The sky was an infinite blank blue.

Soon they came to the land of the *cosecheros*, the tobacco growers of southern Paraguay and northern Argentina. These were mostly small, rented plots of land, where families and *collectivos* arrived with wagonloads of tobacco seedlings. Their plots formed a piecemeal quilt over the plateau.

The boat stopped to trade with merchants who appeared in bark canoes, carrying bundles of *torcidos negros*: tobacco leaves dipped in molasses and twisted into small torpedos. The captain gave each of the emigrants a plug and showed them how to chew it. It's very strong, he said, taking a huge plug for himself, and laughing when they moved away to retch.

In the towns of Nueva Roma, Argerich, Villa Iris Rondeau, Hucal, Perú, Epu-pel, Unanue, and Acha, the Russos found evidence of their ancestors who fled Spain and

Portugal in the 1500s, and came to South America with the first colonialists.

Under the Alhambra Decree of 1492, signed by Queen Isabella, all the Jews of Spain who refused to convert to Christianity were expelled or killed. Many fled to Portugal where, five years later, Princess Isabella of Aragon agreed to marry Manuel I of Portugal on the condition that he follow the politics of the Spanish crown—thus causing the Jews of that country to flee again. Manuel and Isabella were married in October, bringing the Inquisition to a close.

Jews crossed the Atlantic to South America on merchant ships on their way to the Spanish colonies. They joined the communities on the fringes of Spanish and Portuguese colonies on the outskirts of Buenos Aires—escaped slaves, mestizos, deserters, and plains Indians who had learned to herd the wild cattle and horses. They became traders. They travelled in ox carts to Córdoba, bringing yerba maté from Paraguay, wines from Cuyo, and wool and tobacco from Uruguay and Paraguay.

The traces of these earlier European and Russian emigrants were written in the intricate leatherwork of the saddles on which the descendants of those Jews now sat, and who greeted Cohen and the other newcomers with familiarity. Their rigging bore the names of multiple generations of Jewish *gauchos* who had ridden over the plains for the last two hundred years. There were prayers in Hebrew around the pommel and charms in Spanish around the skirt. There were fantastic etchings depicting their histories, one showing a cowboy on horseback blowing a shofar, and perched at the edge of the twisting Río Paraná.

Nathan Cohen and the other emigrants arrived in Moisésville in September of 1901. It was spring. A constant, chill breeze blew, shaking the leaves of big sycamores like rattles. Cottonwoods dispersed their dander and it settled and floated on the river. There were big, stately clouds on the horizon, giants passing by, their huge shadows dousing them in twilight until they passed again and left them in the dazzling spring sunlight. In the distance the Patagonian peaks were tipped with snow.

When Cohen and his party arrived, they were greeted by their former country-people who hailed from all over the Pale. There were many tears, much joy. And—how extraordinary to see the *sukkah* in the fields of young corn, tents made of palm fronds and decorated with *Etrog, lulav, hadass,* and *aravah.* The corn Cohen had left in Russia was five-feet tall and thick with green ears, but here the stalks were barely a foot high. The seasons were reversed. Here, on a balmy spring day, on the fifteenth day of the seventh month of *Tishrei,* in the year 5672, the newcomers were invited to celebrate the harvest-to-come. They recited the prayer for the end of the diaspora:

> Baruch atah, Adonai Eloheinu, Melech haolam, she-hechehyanu, v'kiy'manu, v'higianu laz'man hazeh.

> Blessed are You, Adonai our God, Sovereign of all who has kept us alive, sustained us, and brought us to this season.

Just as the Jews in the Baltic steppes had arrived a thousand years ago, coming to "the bank of a ravine which flows south to the River Bug, and the name of the valley was

Sehaidak, and they found a fertile and rich soil there that was growing a man-tall wild grass, and they began immediately with the construction of the clay houses, kneading the clay with chaff and making bricks in wooden molds which they dried in the sun," so had their children raised a home in the wild desert of Argentina.

They feasted. There were huge asadas of beef and mutton; grilled lamb chorizo and salsa negro. There was borshch with purple potatoes, and carbonada with boiled beef and spring vegetables. There were kreplach and latkes. There were pyrizhky and empanadas: some with chick pea, potatoes, and charred spring onions; others with beef heart or chicken liver. There were more stuffed with quince, pear, mango, apple, or strawberry.

Near midnight, when the moon had risen full, they went down to the river quite drunk and happy. They brought clay urns of maté, and bottles of sukharyky and alfajores. They brought jugs of wine from their own vineyards, tobacco from their fields, and music, such wonderful music. It seemed as if their wandering had ended, and they had sauntered drunk into the Holy land, "Where," as the poet says, "the sun shall shine more brightly than ever he has done, shall perchance shine into our minds and hearts, and light up our whole lives with a great awakening light, as warm and serene and golden as on a bankside in autumn."

That night, Cohen and two others made their beds near the horse paddock. They kept watch, sitting on the bars of the cypress fence, smoking robustos, and passing a bottle of wine. There was no time for sleeping, anyway. It was a perfect night. The bright face of the moon and an ocean of stars.

Constellations lined up across the horizon: Leo followed by Cancer followed by Gemini followed by Taurus followed by Aries. One of the men pointed towards the milky cluster of stars that stretched across the sky: *mborevi rape*. That's what the Guaraní call it. The way of the tapir. You hear them crashing through the scrub at night. If you're lost you can follow them, and they always find water. The man lit another cigar and smoked in silence.

Each of them had come ten thousand miles across oceans, mountains, rivers, and forests to Argentina. If they laid a stone for every step they marched or sailed or dug or plowed, all in the disinterested way one serves the future generations, the path would stretch past the moon. It was the promise of Israel. Yet here before that blank white face, what seemed to connect the two places, Russia to Argentina, Bauska to Moisésville, was space. It was as if the lunar light was a hole in the sky through which the cycles of history spiraled one way and then the other like the ouroboros, the snake eating its tail. What was progress? What did it mean to carry on, or to carry forward?

If they were lucky, the immigrants came with a wife, a husband, children. Others came alone. Most had left their families back in Russia. They left the already dead and the dying. They left homelands that crumbled under irredentist cries of Land, Myth, Religion, Desire. Argentina offered little relief, though the sheer emptiness of the plains and skies paradoxically made it feel small and close and safe.

With the moon so bright, everything was visible; yet the visibility, too, made it particularly empty. The wind carried the sound of the revelers down by the river, the merry music-making, splashing in the water, the pleasant voices of children. The winds wrapped their voices up in a gust and exhaled them beyond the light of the paddock and into the night.

In the early dawn they roused themselves. One man made a fire and then brewed yerba maté. Cohen took a gourd and walked into field of young corn. There were heavy clouds in the distance and the light was ethereal. Away down by the river were the *sukkah* where the revelers from the night before slept in various states of repose. There was another beyond the field of budding flax. The sun crested and the first rays of light shone golden and warm. Birds sang out. The trees buzzed with cicadas.

Las pampas were the edge of the world. From Bauska to Moisésville, Cohen had seen the sweep of the Lord's hand. The thunder in Russia sounded not unlike the thunder in Argentina. The straw was of a different variety, but it slept just the same. Over the *sukkah* in the field, the full moon was sinking west. Its face was cold and distant. Jupiter and Mars, two gods of war, followed after. The horses neighed and stamped. Cohen was already moving towards the paddock where the men were raising saddles. In a blink they swung onto the horses and kicked into trots, the horses pulling, ready to run. After months of travel, he was seated again on the back of a horse, with the edge of creation before him.

In Bauska, in preparation for his journey to Argentina, Cohen had been told about the bloodthirsty *gaucho* cowboys, "whose readiness to shed blood," the Irish explorer Thomas Hutchinson had reported, "constitutes his prominent features; whose first infantile instrument is the knife; and whose first attraction is the pouring out of blood, and the palpitating flesh of expiring animals."

Instead, Cohen met the ancestors of peoples who had existed in las pampas for over twelve thousand years. Until Spanish conquest, the vast steppes were the rangelands of nomadic peoples like the Tehuelche, Puelche, and Querandí, who hunted the grasses for deer, rhea, guanaco, and pigs; and gathered roots and herbs, blended teas and medicines, and followed the great seasons of Patagonia. When the colonial Spanish forts in Buenos Aires came under attack in 1540, the Spaniards fled, setting free thirty-five horses. When they came back forty years later, they reported populations of wild horses in the thousands, and the nomadic peoples had transformed themselves into the great horse-people of the plains.

Cohen found desert valleys that shared in common with the Baltic, his homeland in Russia, a landscape shaped by the quiet flow and retreat of massive polar glaciers. In the fall he saw blooms of purple and yellow hyssop, and he remembered the same pungent smell of onions in the hills outside of Bauska. He rode the big *criollo* horses whose ancestors had come with the Spanish *conquistadores*, and drove cattle across scrubland. Thousands of miles away from Bauska, in the profound emptiness of the desert, he found he knew the landscape and the animals' languages all the same.

There would be a few good years in Argentina. The *gauchos* were legends of folk tales. They roamed free and brave, had their own codes, and slept under the stars. Cohen worked year-long rides across millions and millions of hectares of land. Cows, sheep, horses; foxes, eagles, rhea, puma. When he greeted the sunrise, Cohen recited a short prayer:

> Modeh Modeh anee lefanecha melech chai vekayam, she-he-chezarta bee nishmatee b'chemla, raba emunatecha.

> I offer thanks to You, living and eternal King, for You have mercifully restored my soul within me; Your faithfulness is great.

Before he slept,

> Dulcemente te pido, que me consigas de Dios los favores y gracias de las cuales yo estoy tan necesitado, en las pruebas, en las miserias y en las aflicciones de la vida.

> Sweetly I ask you for favor and grace of which I am so needy, in the trials, the miseries, and the afflictions of life.

FOUR

A FABLE

On September 19, 1783, at the grounds just outside Paris near the Palace of Versailles, the Montgolfier brothers, Joseph-Michel and Jacques-Étienne, launched the world's first "manned" balloon, the *Martial*, in the basket of which which were a rooster, a duck, and a shaggy yellow terrier.

The balloon was made of taffeta wallpaper coated with alum, to prevent it from catching fire. At capacity it measured nine meters in diameter. Around its girth, and against a backdrop of deepest indigo, it displayed all the faces of the Zodiac in gold thread. At the bottom was Hades, the infernal wanderer. He drove a silver chariot between the edges of day and night.

The launch of the *Martial's* quaint menagerie was attended by a crowd of thirteen thousand people, who were tightly packed around a very large podium in a hay field. At the head of the crowd were none other than King Louis XVI and Marie Antoinette, who, within ten years' time, would lose their heads to the guillotine of the French Revolution.

Rum tum-tum, rum tum-tum.

The festivities began with the shuffle of a drum. The crowd fell silent. The brothers shoveled red-hot coals from a brazier and used a large bellows to send the hot smoke into the balloon's canopy. There was a restless hiss, as if a giant were shuffling in his bed, and then the balloon began to inflate. It opened like a flower searching for the morning, turning this way and that, straining against the rope mooring as it blossomed open under the sun. The brothers placed the brazier beneath the canopy, and now the tongues of red fire danced upward, keeping the balloon taught and ready to leap away.

Rum tum-tum, rum tum-tum.

One brother held the duck out towards the King and Queen, while the other one raised the rooster. The crowd cheered. The brothers crated the birds and leashed the dog to the ornate golden railing that circled the basket like a halo.

The duck and rooster squawked. The dog barked. A constable approached a canon near the royal grandstand. He fired it three times, and the brothers cut the tethers. Instantly, the balloon warbled to the sky, then *s t r e t c h* as the airship found the weight of its cargo. *S t r e t c h*, and the basket danced, began to rise—first knee-high, then soon at their shoulders, then their heads. No longer under the spell of gravity, the duck, the rooster, and the dog broke free, and the world's first aeronauts sailed dreamily into the sky.

The crowd was icily quiet as the balloon rose. When it was just a speck three thousand feet above, they went mad. At once, all thirteen thousand people were running, laughing, shouting, delirious, chasing the balloon as it drifted over Versailles, along the winding country roads, and stampeding pastures and fields along the way. The canon fired three more times.

Boom! Boom! Boom!

The *Martial's* flight lasted for eight minutes before the balloon meandered safely back to earth, nearly a mile and a half from where it was released. Among those present at the launch was the poet and scientist Erasmus Darwin, who called out to the fair travelers in his Odes to the Planets which he published the following year:

> Watch, as it rises, the diminish'd sphere.
> —Now less and less—and now a speck is seen;—
> Save him, ye Saints! Who o'er the good preside;
> Bear him ye winds! Ye stars benignant! Guide.
> So Argo, rising from the southern main,
> Lights with new stars the blue ethereal plain;
> With favouring beams the mariner protects,
> And the bold course, which first it steer'd, directs.

The brothers proposed to break the earth's clutch on destiny and let humankind wander unleashed through the stars. Erasmus Darwin made his ode a prayer: "Leave the red eye of Mars on rapid wing," he says. Find peace among the stars.

On that glorious morning, the fearless barnyard pilots became the collective's dream, sailing beyond the fates, and into possibility. Eventually, the explorers were caught by the tug of home. The coal fire dwindled in the thin atmosphere until the last red ember winked to the celestial gods and then was silent. The thinnest wisps of smoke faded into the ether. Gravity overcame their heroic progress, and the balloon began its retreat from the edge of night.

In the celebration that broke out, the brothers were asked why they pursued the fantastic narrative of sending the pastoral crew into the ether. One of the brothers replied, "Well! What is the point of the child who has just been born?" A duck, a rooster, and a dog—the end of the joke is that they drifted safely back to earth to the awaiting hands of their beloved admirers, and into the spill of joy.

—FIVE—
VASARI, 1913—A VISION FROM THE PAST—
WHEN NATHAN COHEN LOST HIS MIND—TWO
SMALL MIRACLES—A NEW OCCUPATION

JULY, 1913. The *Vasari* came within view of Rio de Janeiro's half-moon bay. Cohen had now made the round trip between the continents six times. He was half the way to completing his seventh when two small miracles occurred, and suddenly Nathan Cohen found new employment aboard the ship.

The *Vasari* had pulled into the harbor of the Brazilian capital, and passengers beheld a city saturated and dripping with color. The black sea rose to meet the shore, a jagged line of raw canvas. French colonial houses marched up the hills in geometric blocks of reds, greens, blues, and yellows. Wide, gray boulevards snaked into mist and downpour. The peaks stood like smoky sentinels: Tijuca, Corcovado, Sacopa, Pedra da Gavea. Everywhere there were people. It was hot. The ships in port bobbed in the swell: merchant ships, schooners, naval ships. Men and women beached fishing boats with bamboo gaffing poles. Fish were hauled in alive, bound in heavy driftnets. Glass buoys in intricate abaca macramé hung from the sides of the ships.

The *Vasari* moored in Guanabara harbor. The rains abated near evening and the air hung thick and swampy. Lanterns were lit along the dock. The light refracted in the rain, and the shipyard was awash in a gauze of light. Men unloaded cargo, and cranes swept over the gunwales. Passengers boarded, ferrying their belongings and fighting their way through the crowds, often with children in tow.

"Look out there!"

"Easy now!"

Cargo was loaded into waiting wagons below. Teams of horses set off with a *whip-crack* and *whinny* onto narrowly lit cobblestone streets, *clop clop clopity clop*. Cohen was led to the docks to present his papers. He said a few words to the official in mangled Spanish, or perhaps it was Portuguese. It was the spit of a madman, though some life still trickled from his lips like expectation. The magistrate denied his appeal, and Cohen returned to the ship.

He joined the boarding passengers and then broke off towards the main cargo hold. The crew had begun loading the livestock that waited noisily in the corrals on the dock. Cohen rested his elbows on the wooden fencing and watched the cattle stomping and snorting in the murky light.

At nine the ship's bells rang. Porters called for any final ticketholders to come aboard. The last of the animals were being corralled, and it was then that Cohen beheld the first of the miracles. He was struck by a specter: three big *criollo* horses mixed in with a group of roans and pintos. The brands on the *criollo* were uniform: two interlaced eights on the horses' flanks with antlered serifs. There was no mistaking the white patches like witches' hands, blurred sideways on one horse, long and jagged on another. This was where they had been touched by an ancient magic summoned by the Waki people, Dr. Solanet had said.

North of Moisésville, in the small town of Ayacucho, outside of Santa Fe, was the hacienda of the well-known veterinarian, Dr. Emilio Solanet, whose main hobby was the native horses of Patagonia. Because the animals had only come to the New World with the *conquistadores*, they made for a fascinating and observable case for Darwin's theories of evolution. Within the span of a few hundred years there had arisen marked differences in the horses of Patagonia, for example, from those in the mountains of Peru.

It was Dr. Solanet whom Nathan Cohen worked for, when Cohen first arrived in Moisésville in 1901—first as a stable boy, and then as a *gaucho*, driving cattle across the great plains. Solanet was especially interested in the *criollo*, the big workhorses of the pampas. The horses' forebears had been traded amongst the Waki peoples since the first of the horses arrived with the *conquistadores* on the shores of what would later become Brazil. The Tehuelche peoples had bred the animals to be hard and tough like Patagonia. Se dedicó a rescatar los valores del caballo criollo, Solanet said. They shall be preserved.

Solanet's ranch was nestled among the iron-red hills of Santa Fe. The long, low hacienda was a gleaming swath of white plaster, blanketed with mosaic roofs of crimson tile. Pepper and carob trees shaded courtyards, and granite paving stones followed desire lines along sparkling pools filled with trout. There was a greenhouse devoted to rare orchids. The saddles in the stables had been passed down by Spanish ancestors who had known personally or had had intimate dealings with the likes of Ruy López de Villalobos, and Francisco Hernández de Córdoba, the first of the great Spanish explorers.

Cohen worked for Solanet for a little over seven years. Then, against admonitions and warnings from his employer, he took his savings north across the Atlantic to the United States. He sailed to New York, then traveled south by train to the panhandle of Florida, where he and a cousin invested their savings in a mucking scheme, buying a parcel of land in Apalachicola. Under governor Napoleon Bonaparte Broward, it seemed as if the entire peninsula would soon be drained for cane and tobacco. Timber companies felled the cypress, pine, and mahogany groves, and canneries were founded daily. Hunters and collectors ravaged the jungle for alligator, waterfowl, and rare flowers. Cohen and his cousin planned to breed the *criollo* workhorses of Patagonia to pull wagons and plows through the saw grass in the civilizing service of agriculture.

However, when Nathan Cohen arrived in Apalachicola, he found a sleepy oyster hamlet, and lands of bogs and sand dunes. There was no mucking scheme. There were no lands to be civilized unless the swamps were first drained, and from the look of things that was a long way away. Nathan's cousin had already vamoosed. After spending a week there, and finding himself the near-victim to two petty larcenies, as well as a run-in with a cottonmouth snake (a man shot the snake from twenty paces while Cohen looked on, not dumbfounded, just interested), Cohen found transportation back to Jacksonville and spent the last of his money on a train ticket back to New York.

Before he left, Cohen penned a short letter to Dr. Solanet, telling him that the scheme had failed. He boarded the Seaboard Air Railway Line in Jacksonville in late 1911. Somewhere along the way, Cohen suffered a nervous breakdown and fled the train.

Some weeks later Nathan Cohen was found in Baltimore, sleeping in an abandoned warehouse. When his person was searched very little turned up. In one pocket was his original ticket on the *Vasari* from Argentina to New York. The signature at the bottom was the only thing that named him. There was some loose change in his shoe, and a clay vessel with an ancient Hebrew script in his lapel. All the items were placed in a paper sack and sewn to the hem of Cohen's coat. He was cataleptic, rigid, and unresponsive. They dragged him from the warehouse and placed him in a wagon amongst a swag of derelicts, drunks, and the near or possibly dead.

Cohen was impounded in an asylum until he could be deported

> as one of the classes of aliens that shall be excluded from admission into the United States: all idiots, imbeciles, feebleminded persons, epileptics, insane persons, and persons who have been insane within five years previous; persons who have had two or more attacks of insanity at any time previously; paupers; persons likely to become a public charge; professional beggars; persons afflicted with tuberculosis or with a loathsome or dangerous contagious disease; and persons not comprehended within any of the foregoing excluded classes who are found to be and are certified by the examining surgeon as being mentally or physically defective, such mental or physical defect being of a nature which may affect the ability of such alien to earn a living…

—so said The Immigration Act of 1907, passed by the 59th Congress and signed into law by President Theodore Roosevelt.

Nathan Cohen was expelled from the United States in April 1912. He sailed on the *Vasari*, not knowing the ship would become his permanent home. It was the same ship he arrived on when he traveled from Argentina to New York a year earlier. In his third-class bunk-room were seven other men who played cards, sang songs, and spoke about work and food in native tongues that formed a babel of speech, though everyone was perfectly understood—all except Nathan Cohen, whom they avoided with unabashed intensity.

One by one, the men debarked at ports along the South American coast, and one by one they were replaced with other men who spoke in similarly unruly tongues, fidgeted with hunting knives, polished their boots, and discussed amongst themselves their various work contracts, reading and rereading them aloud, comparing the particulars of the job advertisements and letters, and noting how much money could really be made owing to the various company stores, the thieves and bandits, and death.

At Buenos Aires, the ship's steward brought Cohen before yet another magistrate in yet another of the immigration offices. He explained that Cohen had been evicted from the United States and was being returned to his port of origin. His original ticket—stamped Buenos Aires, Argentina, 1911—was presented to the magistrate as proof; his scrawled signature at the bottom indicating he was "Natan" or maybe "Nothan," "Cohen" or "Koan," or something altogether different.

Who was he? Another unworthy immigrant. A lunatic who presented certain dangers to the good citizens of Argentina. A black-haired Jew with a long beard and a halo of sickness.

No, they said. Without papers, or anything that said he was, in fact, an Argentinean citizen, or a citizen of any other country for that matter, the request to debark was denied. Cohen was returned to the *Vasari*. He would be shipped back to the United States, where he might await further developments.

A year and a half had passed since Cohen had discovered the swampy acres in Apalachicola and knew that everything was gone. He had gone back and forth between North and South America almost seven times, and only lately had he awoken into the mists of a transparent present. And now, as the *Vasari* readied for departure from Rio de Janeiro, blowing its long, heavy foghorn in salute, there in the wet twilight of the stables, Cohen found his kin. Amongst those animals were three *criollo* with Dr. Solanet's own brand.

Cohen was so startled when he saw the horses that he was tempted to place his hand on the mark where they had been marked by the Waki, just as Solanet had done, but he refrained. He let the symbol go unexplained. Even without touching them, Cohen knew these were the brothers and sisters of those same horses he had known back in Moisésville. All three wore Dr. Solanet's personal brand. He followed behind the animals like a sleepwalker.

That night, the *Vasari* departed Rio for New York. For the next three weeks, Cohen spent whatever time he could below with the animals. He filled his pockets with scraps and peels from the galleys to feed the horses and conversed with them as old friends.

For the entire first year of Cohen's existence aboard the ship, the crew had not heard Cohen say anything. After that night, if the sailors crept into the stables near twilight, they might spy Cohen atop the corral's wooden beams, a low gruff song spilling from beneath his beard.

At other times he was quiet, bemused, deep in thought. He pulled at his beard. He sputtered silent questions and protests. He held his face in his two fists, and his eyes were closed. Meanwhile the horses kicked and stamped. They chewed and kvetched. They took the scraps from his hands, turning their big muzzles sideward to delicately nip the peels and straw from his hand.

After a few blessed weeks, the *Vasari* came within sight of New York Harbor, and Cohen readied to say goodbye to the horses. Perhaps this was the hardest thing he had yet to do as there was little hope the chance to see his kinfolk would come again. Nevertheless, while the *Vasari* was outfitted for its next southernly voyage, the second small miracle occurred.

One of the foremen came up behind Cohen and put his hand on Cohen's shoulder and led him to the corrals just off the main hold. The foreman showed Cohen the air vents and the cooling ducts, which Cohen would be responsible for sweeping out three times a day. He showed him the water supply, where it disconnected, where it was apt to get clogged, and how to syphon the water out and clean the hoses. He showed him the storage bins, where they kept baling tools and forks, and the haylofts. All of this was done without a word. The foreman simply pointed, and Cohen nodded his head. The foreman also showed Cohen a space in the rafters where he might make a bed. Other men would sometimes snooze there. Cohen would make it his home.

Cohen began work at once. He retrieved a soap bucket and took a sponge to a trough, kneeling amongst the animals as he cleaned. He hummed as he worked. He climbed a rope ladder and wiped the fans and the ventilation ducts. He polished the bulbs that hung over each of the stalls. He cleaned the water supply and drank the cold tap water. In the morning he crawled across the gangway and dropped fresh hay into the stalls and then began again.

Gradually grew the possibility of carrying on. There was work to do, and there didn't seem to be any question that his lot had been cast, that he never would escape the limbo of the high seas. When the crew departed at the last ship's bell, he climbed to the loft, removed his boots, and fell asleep. A sliver of moonlight showed through narrow slats in the hatchway that led out of the corrals.

* * *

To the Jews who wandered in Canaan, the Lord commanded His children to first make Him a gift: of gold, silver and copper; blue, purple and crimson yarn, fine linen and goats' hair; rams' skins dyed red, dolphin skins, and acacia wood; oil for lighting, spices for the oil of anointing and for aromatic incense; lapis lazuli and precious setting stones for the ephod and the breast piece. "Have them make Me a holy place," the Lord said to Moses, "and I will dwell in their midst."

Without considering the consequences, or perhaps even the *why*, Cohen, too, began to collect raw materials that he found as he swabbed the decks: silk, thread, buttons, rope, skins, oil, spars, planks, cotton, and nails. He pocketed lost items, things, detritus, and trash. He kept all this in a box that he hid in the hay at the foot of his bed, until eventually the fragments might serve some purpose. At night he burned incense that he made from smudges of tar and perfume, and which swirled around his head as he prayed late into the night.

Spying the light coming from Nathan Cohen's bunk in the hayloft, gleaming through the wooden gates of the corrals, as caught in the long view of, say, a landscape painting, which has captured the *Vasari* steaming on ahead in the dead of night, one might be struck by Cohen's tiny lamp, the "sort of indefinite, half-attained, unimaginable sublimity about it," as the poet says. If one perseveres, eventually one loses interest in the ship entirely—that "black mass of something hovering in the center of the picture." Only that single point of illumination remains. As one begins to perceive, the light matters, because it is temporary. Soon it will disappear forever. As soon as one grows attached to the warm light heart, it slips from your grasp and then is gone.

SEPTEMBER, 1913—THE OPERA SINGER AND HER DOG—A PERFORMANCE—A FEUDAL VISION

SEPTEMBER, 1913. Newspapers reported "50 Blown Up!" after Mexican rebels planted dynamite under railroad tracks south of Saltillo. Forty Federal soldiers, and ten second-class passengers, were the official dead. The number of injured was not given. The train was looted, and the surviving passengers were robbed.

In the capital, in Mexico City, as relations with the US grew ever tenser, it was reported that "fewer of the lower classes, who are usually much in evidence at the bullfights, attended today. This was said to be due to the fact that recruiting officers are taking advantage of such gatherings to swell the ranks of the army. The bands played in the parks, which were filled with the usual Sunday crowds."

Across the Atlantic Ocean, the first of the Balkan Wars ended when Adrianople was taken by the Greek armies, sounding the death knell of the Ottoman Empire. The "Exalted Ottoman State," which had been founded by Sultan Osman the First in 1299, had lasted for six hundred years.

"It will be a dry-eyed funeral," reported one newspaper. "The records of Turkish rule in Europe are one long catalogue of bloodshed and rapine, at first directed by the genius of one of the most remarkable dynasties which the world has seen, but never from first to last inspired by the faintest traditions of culture...The rose garden replaces the dung-hill, and flourishing modern cities the foul and moldering hamlets of a century ago...The proverb which declares that grass does not grow where the Ottoman hoofs have trod merely gives poetical expression to a fact which is as indisputable as the law of gravity."

In Bohemia, in the capital city of Prague, and in the same garret where Franz Kafka will soon write his masterpiece, *Das Schloss*, the famed seer Madame de Thèbes made her yearly predictions, published as a notice pasted outside her house at Zlatá ulička 14. She issued the following proclamations:

War will continue to menace the world, as the planet Mars will predominate throughout the year.

A terrible catastrophe is predicted in London. The city will be threatened by floods as a result of inundations.

The monarchy will be restored in Portugal.

Profound changes amounting to a political up-heaval will take place in Germany and the national life of that nation will be completely transformed.

In California, the state legislature passed the Alien Land Law, which "prohibited aliens ineligible for citizenship from owning agricultural land or possessing long-term leases over it, but permitted leases lasting up to three years." "Aliens ineligible for citizenship" was a coded reference to the 1870 Naturalization Act, which extended citizenship to African Americans but not specifically to any other racial groups. California used the ambiguity to target Japanese and Chinese immigrants. The Expatriation Act, for instance, provided that "any woman marrying an alien ineligible for citizenship shall cease to be an American citizen," making marriages to *issei* impossible.

In response to the passing of the Alien Land Law, there were widespread protests in California and also in Japan, where fomented a deep resentment against the United States. Japan had soundly beaten Russia in the war of 1904, but the Portsmouth Treaty, presided over by Theodore Roosevelt, who won a Nobel Peace Prize for his efforts, treated Japan and Russia as equal adversaries. Although the protests were mostly peaceful, still there was reason for concern. As one editor opined: "Although sensible people are not disposed to become excited over the agitation which has been caused in Japan by the California Alien Land Law, or fear a possible war with that country as a result, it serves every useful purpose to carefully consider what such a war would mean and to take stock of our means and resources for meeting such an emergency."

* * *

Cohen's loft in the corrals was in the rear of the ship with the cargo hold. Soot from the smokestacks blanketed the stables and every day Cohen woke with grit in his throat and his teeth. Forward the chimney stacks were the first-class cabins, which rose above the deck four stories above the waterline.

These caught only the fresh ocean breeze, although there was an army of maids that continuously swept and dusted, which was how Cohen himself had become a sweeping nonentity aboard the ship. Elite passengers could rent private rooms for themselves and their families to make use of during the long hours of the voyage. Many of the cabins were ruled over by nannies in charge of three or four children in matching bow ties and wool sailor pants. The youngest child raced toy trains across a heavily carpeted floor while his older sibling lay prone with a book in her hand beneath the shelter of an oak table, gilt-edged and hand-carved, and with a provenance dating back to the Widow of Windsor, while her spirit was off on the adventures of Jo March one day, the Man in the Iron Mask, Mattie Ross, or Anne Shirley the next.

Best of all, however, were the cabins with windows that faced forward. At four stories up in the air, a body pressed against the plate-glass window would have had nothing to block her view of the limitless road of ocean that sped towards her at almost fourteen knots, until the nannie caught her at the window and took her down, wagging her finger, *tsk*ing "child, child," though the little girl looked on over her shoulder wistfully.

Sometimes the cabins were rented for the rehearsal of private transactions that might take place in open waters. Occasionally there were rumors of poker games and the like, though the staff took great pains to deny such whispers.

And sometimes a room might be rented by a single, glorious personage, as was the case with the one occupied by the opera singer Salomé Amvrosiivka Krushelnytska, and in whose darkened corner, on that warm September morning in 1913, in a green royal chaise lounge, reclined the young painter Tarsila do Amaral, who had boarded the *Vasari* two days before on her way to New York. Later Tarsila would go on to Berlin where some of her new paintings were to be shown.

Do Amaral had, coincidentally, spied Nathan Cohen when she boarded the ship. She paused to watch the men load the horses, and Cohen came down the gangplank with a bit of rope in one hand. He was a weird, unshapely man in a tattered, black wool coat and hat, with a long beard and sunken eyes. He brushed by Tarsila again when she entered the hall to the first-class cabins; he excused himself with a grunt as he passed. He continued on his way and joined the other crew in loading the horses as if he were one of them.

Tarsila drew in a palm-sized sketchbook with a piece of charcoal. Her father had given it to her as a present for the voyage. The cover was soft black leather, and the stitching on the spine raw gray silk. She thumbed back through the first few pages—brief depictions of the passengers, sailors hauling cargo, animals in the corrals...Tarsila's eyes wandered from the paper to the woman seated at the dressing table—Salomé Amvrosiivka Krushelnytska herself—to the little phantom of a dog, sleeping on a silk cushion beneath the woman's chair— "Laika," Salomé called the dog. Around the dog's neck was a silver chain that glinted in the light. At the center hung a teardrop of lapis lazuli.

Tarsila's eye drifted to the curtained window and to the theatrical fresco that covered the ceiling. Angels bathed along the banks of the Amazon river, and ibises, macaws, owls, contigas, topaz, oropendolas, and parrots perched above them in the trees. Kites, eagles, and the "flying jewel" of the sky, the kingfisher, circled in the skies above, and dolphin and loggerhead turtles skirted a white-washed riverboat that chugged upriver. Tarsila looked down at her paper and with her finger blurred a charcoal line into shadow.

There was a symbolic harmony to the room that made everything significant, and likewise made the room enchanting, but mostly the unity made the room maddening for Tarsila to draw. Everything was staged. All avenues of possibility had been curtailed and nothing was left to chance. If there was a line of flight, she could not find it.

For example: Heavy red curtains obscured the large port window. The walls were a sour yellow with teak wainscoting. There was a gilt chair, padded in saffron tucked into a writing desk, and a filigree card rack, hanging from a blue ribbon on a brass knob, with five or six visiting cards. On top of a teak dressing table, inlaid with marble and jade, were delicate cut-glass bottles of perfume, and an antique vase with a single lily; a silvery wig perched on a mannequin head; and there was a small chest whose open drawers were filled with tins of rouge, tint, lipstick, and powders. Added to that litany of oscuros was the heavy smoke of incense, which, filtered through candlelight, made the salon a magic lantern of moving shadows. Instead of real life, Krushelnytska invoked the visions of a spiritualist.

Tarsila put the piece of charcoal back into a paper box and tied a leather strap around her sketchbook. On the table was a stack of newspapers: La Nación, La Prensa, Le Matin,

The Times, and Pravda. On top, one page had been folded in half so that the headline was visible: "8,000 in Great Suffrage March." The story continued below the headline: "Nearly three miles of New Yorkers doubled in ranks ten deep got a new idea about votes for women yesterday afternoon, when between 8,000 and 9,000 suffragists marched from Washington Square north on Fifth avenue to Carnegie Hall."

Tarsila shifted the newspapers. Beneath them was a Tarot, dealt in the shape of a cross. Only two of the cards had been turned over. In the center was The Empress. Before her was The Fool. The other cards lay faces down with their backs turned. The reverse sides of the cards showed elaborate geometric mosaics.

Like the newspapers that covered it, the Tarot was another set piece in a room full of set pieces. It had been waiting to be read, a red plot-line carefully laid out like a herring trap. The Tarot promised that deeper meanings would be set adrift in the smoky, already opaquely storied room. The Tarot was deliberate, which meant that something was being imposed on her. Tarsila might have resented the imposition if she didn't also find it grotesquely alluring, like a dream almost remembered.

The Empress must have stood for Krushelnytska. The card depicted a queenly figure seated on a throne. Her robes were silver and gold, and in her right hand she held a scepter. Her other hand rested on the head of a stork. Her crown was a band of silver with an aquamarine stone in the center.

Across the room was The Empress in the flesh. She was seated in a gilt chair at her dressing table, preparing to dazzle the *Vasari*'s passengers. Her crow-black hair was streaked with pearl and plaited and tied above her head. Through the tight bun was a spike of silver inlaid with diamonds. Her gown was a deep royal plum trimmed with stardust. She hummed a Ukrainian folk tune from her native Lviv, Nich yaka misiachna, zoriana, yasnaia, Vydno, khoch holky zbyrai. The night, O Lord, moon lit, star light; so bright a pin we could find.

She was at the peak of her powers.

The dignified Empress contrasted blatantly with The Fool, the one who would cross her path. The Fool's is the only card without a number. Some call it zero, but the history of the card predates zero's invention. The mosaics on the backs of the cards, for example, came from the far-older Qur'anic principles of Tawhid and Mizan, unity and balance. The Fool was dressed in rags. A crescent moon hung over his shoulder. He wore a hat made of straw, and a little dog nipped at his heels.

A knock at the door drew Tarsila's attention away. Her father had come to retrieve her. It was an hour before Krushelnytska would sing for the ship's guests, and he wanted to introduce Tarsila to another artist, Anita Malfatti, who had recently been in Berlin. Tarsila rose, and as she did so she turned the third card: The Magician, whose number is I. Tarsila laughed. If she was to play the role of *le bateleur*, the singularity, the point from which all possibility emerges—then what? But at that moment Krushelnytska touched her arm. "My dear" she said, "I must dress. Thank you for your company." In return, Tarsila thanked Krushelnytska for the quiet afternoon, curtsied as one does before a grand person, and excused herself.

A half hour later, Tarsila do Amaral sat with a host of passengers in their most formal of formalwear, in the first-class music conservatory on the upper promenade deck, awaiting the arrival of Salomé Amvrosiivka Krushelnytska. Waiters hurried between the guests, their trays laden with beer and wine. The light in the chandelier flickered like gaslighting. "A faint blue haze of cigar smoke rose from all corners of the room," as they say. "The smell of gas mingled with people's breath; the breeze from the portholes whisked it away."

When Krushelnytska finally glided through the ranks of passengers, she trailed a sea of sequins. When she sat, the silver played a concerto of light over the dazzled crowd. She bowed her head and thanked her guests, and then a steward read from the opening summary of Wagner's *Lohengrin*. The steward cleared his throat, then: "Hungarian marauders harass the federated German tribes, and the long-suffering kingdom is poised to defend its ancestral homelands." Et cetera, et cetera.

The lights in the salon dimmed. Krushelnytska, aglitter in candlelight, began a gentle, almost silent aria. It swept forth like a vision, drawing for the passengers a windswept night, a Gothic vision from long ago. The chill of Krushelnytska's voice brushed over Tarsila's skin, suggesting a memory she knew but couldn't touch.

The entire ship dreamt into Wagner's Aryan past inside Krushelnytska's soprano. Just outside the salon, passengers who couldn't secure an invitation to the performance sat on benches and in loungers, rapt in the melodies of longing. On the second- and third-class decks, passengers gathered around radio-boxes over which the performance was broadcast. Tears were wiped away and hands were clasped. In the clutches of that feudal vision, the voyagers of the *Vasari* became the chorus of the citizens of Brabant. These were the brothers of the mythological German tribes, the flesh grown up from the ancient Bavarian soil. This was their homeland. They stood like a march of sunflowers, listening to the longing tale of their queen as she pled for her life. And where was her champion?

"There!" someone shouted.

"What draws near in the light of the moon?"

"See! See! What a strange and wondrous sight!"

"A swan? A swan is drawing a boat here! A knight is standing upright in it! How brightly shines his armor! My eye is dazzled by its gleam!"

"See, he is already drawing nearer! The swan draws him by a golden chain!"

"See, still nearer he comes towards the shore!"

"Behold him! He comes!"

Truly, they saw the knight boarding the *Vasari* in his clanking, shining armor, ready to defend Elsa's honor. The last notes crescendoed with longing and dissolved into expectation. The second- and third-class passengers cheered. The more elevated guests in the salon were quiet, stunned and devoted. Then they too clapped, and Krushelnytska rose and took a bow. She sat again. And then again floated an airy, wandering tune, which steered Tarsila and the rest of the passengers further along the edge of dream.

A HOLE IN TIME—COHEN REVISITS HIS PAST— ILLUMINATION—THE DOG IN THE LAMPLIGHT

BELOW DECKS, the horses had stopped their chewing and their cramped movements, their snorting and braying and reluctant stamping. The stacks of crated birds and other animals went silent too. Nothing moved. Nothing whispered. Cohen graffitied the lines of a river into a beam above his bed in the rafters using a nib he'd fashioned from a splinter of steel. The stillness washed over the ship, and he put his scribe into its sheath and climbed down.

Except for the animals, the stables and cargo hold were empty. Cohen walked through the dark, knowing every opaque form he passed as an old friend, patting a muzzle here, adjusting a feed bag there. At the rear of the stable he swung back an oaken door, and taking a lantern from a peg, he made his way into the warren of the cargo hold. Mice scurried, and a cat chased one away into the dark. He walked to the scaffolding of stairs and climbed into the sting of sea air and hazy deck-light.

It was a balmy evening. The moon came and went through heavy black clouds. Its wolfish face flashed lupine scars, then it was gone. Krushelnytska's voice broadcast from the foredeck, just beyond the entrance to the cargo hold. Shipmates had gathered to listen at the base of a radio-box and warmed themselves in its glow. Song joined with the perpetual rushing of wind and sea, the night screeches of the gulls, the deep churning of the engines, and the billowing smoke. On the first-class promenade at the forward deck, the music conservatory was aglow with flickering lights. Passengers outside had gathered like spellbound moths. The ship rushed on, guided by the wistful notes.

Then the ship came into fog. The voice of Elsa canted like a mechanical dream. The lamentations of the future queen of Bavaria were ethereal through the tin-pan speakers, and a vision came to Nathan Cohen in the feudal, crackling aria. Buried in Elsa's song was another melody that Cohen had heard many years ago, when he was a boy in Bauska, from a woman he had seen one night in the mists of the silent river.

Cohen and his father had been plowing a potato field along the edge of the Daugava, south of Riga. He was sixteen. In just over a year he would be leaving Riga for Argentina, and he would never see his parents, or this countrside, again.

Cohen's father had loaded a cart with barrels of water to hold the moldboard and share steady and deep. Cohen sat atop surveying the furrows. He jumped down to scramble for a stone, a piece of wood, or scout ahead for other debris. The huge workhorses lumbered forward tracing the gently sloping contours of the river valley.

As the soil was turned, it revealed its mysteries. Cohen often found old bronze coins eaten with rust, sometimes bits of silver, rarely any gold. He found bones with tears of old clothing still attached. He found miscellaneous teeth. He found potsherds, glass, spoons. Once he found a mezuzah with its seal broken. He examined the clay vessel for its nicks and particularities. It was rare that clay escaped the jaws of the plow unscathed, yet here was a little miracle. Later he inscribed his own little prayer *klaf*, made from a scrap of paper.

The plow excavated ancient worlds, and brought them to the surface where they no longer fit. Cohen and his father found broken timber and bent iron. Russian, Roman, Ottoman, Mongol. Riga was a great crossroads. Sown throughout the valley were the relics of peoples after peoples. They left traces of commerce and war. War and more war. Cohen's father had an ancient dagger that he kept in a bedroom drawer. He polished the broken blade so that it almost shined, would almost reflect his face. The hilt he replaced with spruce, and carved with a star of David. The forged metal was a thousand years old.

They even found part of a mast, which at first they took to be a tree branch. Worst of the unseen dangers to a plow, a spar of wood could be buried for tens of thousands of years, nothing whatsoever to be seen of it above ground, and then one day fate gambles the branch's massive leverage against the blind head of a spade, the release pin is broken, and the plow falls dead to the earth, unhitched. They could lose half a day's work that way.

They dug out the huge splinter, which was almost six feet long. Termites had inscribed their wordless writing, maybe an epitaph of names of the boat's ancient sailor. A ship! In the middle of a field! They loaded the mast onto the cart, and later they used it to frame part of a barn.

That year they'd plowed for potatoes two feet deep. Next year they'd go a little farther down. An inch of strata was another history. Yet the earth seemed only to reveal realms of loss. Nothing remained of the vast kingdoms over which kings once said, "Look on my Works, ye Mighty, and despair!"

Cohen and his father finished plowing long after sunset. Gloom rolled in from the Baltic. They pulled the plugs on the barrels of water and led the horses to pasture. Then a figure approached on horseback, spurred out of the night in great clops of thunder. Cohen heard the hooves first, then saw the rider. The man drew closer and Cohen's father hailed him, Guten tag! The man dismounted and he and Cohen's father shook hands.

The man wore a heavy, black wool hat and a wide woven sash. The sash was patterned with red suns on an alternating white-and-black background, and fine blue zigzags crossing throughout. Underneath the man's cloak flashed a wide bronze belt. Cohen's father and the man exchanged greetings, then walked towards the newly plowed field. Already they were deep in conversation.

Cohen followed behind. He took a fist-sized magnet from his pocket and dropped it to the ground. It remained attached to Cohen's hand by a leather strap. As Cohen walked along he drew the magnet through the freshly plowed furrows, listening for the familiar *clink* of metal snapping against metal. Sometimes he pulled the magnet up like a fishing line having caught an ancient musket ball, an iron screw, or some other scrap.

After the better part of an hour Cohen's father and the man paused. They shook hands again and kissed each other. The man came to Nathan and smiled and shook his hand too and kissed him on the head. ¡Vaya con Dios! He mounted his horse and charged north.

Cohen's father stood before him. He looked him in the eye. The fire made his father's eyes dance a little. He smiled. Meyn zun, he said. In dray yar, ir vet arumforn. Argentine. Zey zogn di ferd bist sheyn.

Nathan, his father said, would work for a year at the *shul* at Beth Midrash, in Žeimelis, twenty kilometers to the south. The rabbis of the synagogue had business all over the Pale. They had a stable of fine horses that they kept in use. Cohen would assist the farriers by shoeing horses, filing nails, doing simple blacksmithing, and caring for the tack and equipment. He would also work in the fields, a bounty of wheat and flax, potatoes, beets, and turnips, which was overseen by the Beth Midrash congregation. In the morning and evening, he would attend services.

The chief rabbi was Abraham Isaac Hakohen Kook, a Nazarite, who kept a strict vegetarian diet, never drank wine, and never cut his hair. He was a deeply respected Torah scholar and kabbalist, and an adherent of the *sefirot*, the mystical branch of Judaism collected under the *Zohar*. Later, Cohen would hear whispers that the great HaRav possessed original fragments of the spell the Ba'al Shem cast to summon the golem.

In Bauska, his father said, things were only getting worse. After a year Nathan would emigrate to a kibbutz in Moisésville in Argentina. They needed young men like Nathan who could handle the horses and knew plows. They called the young men *gauchos*, cowboys. He'd earn good wages.

Would his father and mother be going? No. This was Nathan's opportunity. His father would continue to work, to save money, and one day Nathan's father and mother might join him. But not now. And probably not for many years.

On their way back to Bauska, Cohen and his father passed through the ruined castle at Lenneivarden and made camp on the banks of the Ekau. These were the same shores on which the Prussian troops bivouacked in 1812, preventing Napoleon's troops from moving north to the city. There too, on October 14, 1915, only months after Cohen launched the airship from the *Vasari*, German armies would arrive. On the morning of the following day, they would ford the Ekau at Grunwald, about fifteen miles east of Mitau. A two-day battle would follow for the railroad stations of Garrosen Gross Ekau. There would be several days of hard fighting, and by October 20, the Germans would manage to break through the Russian line.

That night, camping on the banks of the river, Cohen woke to the sound of a woman singing. He rose from his shift and walked down to the riverbank. The fog came and went. The river appeared in stark moonlight, then disappeared into black.

At first there was only the melody, the woman's voice caught in the fog. Then a small raft appeared, making silvery tracks in the slick of water.

The boat was glossed in a corona of light. It floated closer. The woman stood in the rear, holding a wooden rudder steady and true. She wore a royal crimson headscarf, which folded into black robes that were marred by night and fog. Her face was hidden. By her side was a dagger. The dramatic shadows made her a queen. The honey flame of a lantern hung from a pole made her an ascetic, a monk.

By her side was a large black dog with black curly hair. It was a wolfhound, the kind they used to herd sheep in the mountains. The dog was hard to spy as it blended so well into the black river and the black night. It seemed like the lantern had no effect on it. The woman sang verses from the Song of Songs:

> For behold, the winter has passed,
>
> The rain has departed, gone.
>
> The blossoms appear in the land,
>
> The time of singing has arrived.
>
> The voice of the turtledove is heard in our land.
>
> The fig-tree perfumes its young fruit,
>
> And the vines in bud, they give forth fragrance;
>
> Arise, my darling, my beautiful, and go forth.

The woman sang the lines like a caress. With her free hand she channeled the firelight, bringing radiance to her hooded face. "Have you seen him whom my soul loves?" she asked.

In the Song of Songs, the Lover makes his search on a palanquin carved from the cedars of Lebanon, the wood of the tree that "was so tall its top was among the clouds"; the woman made her chariot from the splintered ribs of a derelict whaler. The bony spars had been fleshed out with a thousand small things, a patchwork of boxes, barrels, planks, scavenged lumber, a broken paddlewheel. It was "a spectre, a ghost ship... made from rags and rope and lumber, a vessel from the end of the world, something medieval, the flagship of nothingness." And in the dark night of the unknown, the flame that burned by the woman's side made its own sanctuary of light, burning away all doubt that her lover was there.

The boat passed slowly, and only then did Cohen notice that it left no reflection on the water. The moon's face showed fully upon that mirror, but there was no trace of the craft.

As if replenished and full of new purpose, the little boat slipped into an eddy and vanished into the murk and gloom. In its wake were the heavy perfumes of cedar and frankincense.

Cohen awoke from the dream. Across from the stables, the promenade deck was deserted. The radio box where the passengers had gathered let out a faint hiss. A rolling patch of fog tumbled through the light. When it cleared there was a little shaggy dog at the deck railing. The full face of the moon showed. The dog stared across at him. Her ears were like taught triangles and she had a pearly white beard. She wagged her tail, waiting. Although only twenty meters away, there was the gulf of the cargo hold between them. She turned her head. Beyond was more sea, more stars, more black water. His gaze went back to the spot across the deck where the dog had been but she was gone. Eventually he went to find her.

SALOMÉ AMVROSIIVKA KRUSHELNYTSKA RETURNS TO HER DRESSING ROOM—LAIKA'S DISAPPEARANCE—TWO INCIDENTS WITH THE SHIP'S DETECTIVES—DO AMARAL IS LEFT TO CONTEMPLATE THE EMPTY ROOM

WHEN SALOMÉ AMVROSIIVKA KRUSHELNYTSKA RETURNED TO HER DRESSING ROOM TO CHANGE, she did not, at first, notice that Laika was missing. The hallway outside buzzed with activity. First-class passengers gathered for swanky afterparties in private lounges. She swept gallantly past them, bluster and cigar smoke following her into the room. Inside she was distracted by two porters delivering flowers from Captain Cadogan. They were huge bouquets commissioned in Rio: a rainbow of orchids, Brazilian candle flowers, anthurium, bougainvillea, and lantana.

A maid waited inside for her directions. The porters were dismissed, the door was closed, and after a few quick designations, her attendant went to work. She undid Krushelnytska's gown and hung it on a paneled screen. Krushelnytska sat before the dressing-table mirror and her attendant unpinned her heavy plaits. Krushelnytska let one of her sequined heels fall to the floor, and stretched her toe to nuzzle the dog's fur, but her toe swatted only the thick damask rug.

Then a porter rapped on the door. In his arms were more flowers, and bottles of champagne that dripped with icy chill. Salomé ignored him, calling for the dog instead. "Laika! Laika!" she called. She snapped her fingers. "Laika! Laika!"

There was another knock on the door and Tarsila do Amaral entered. She carried three white roses in one hand, and a bottle of cachaça in the other. "I've brought you rum," she said with a smile. "We make it from our own sugarcane. What is the matter?"

"Laika," Krushelnytska said. "She's gone! She could be anywhere. I don't know how she got out."

"Shall I call for..." Tarsila began to ask but Salomé interrupted her.

"Yes! Please do."

Tarsila opened the door and found a crewman outside. She told him the dog was missing, and to please fetch someone who could help.

Tarsila asked if she should leave but Krushelnytska implored her to sit. "How could she have gotten out?"

Krushelnytska paced the room. She opened the door to look this way and that down the hall, closed it, and continued pacing. Tarsila thumbed through the newspapers on the tea table. The Tarot had been gathered and stored in a silver case, which sat at the corner of the table. Tarsila opened the case and ran her hand along the crushed velvet lining. Face up was the Knave.

Then the ship's detective arrived. Krushelnytska described Laika, though the information was redundant. Krushelnytska often went on deck with her, and many in the crew had grown fond of the dog.

The detective left, but he was soon called back again in even greater haste. "The sketchbook!" Krushelnytska cried. "What has become of it?"

Tarsila had left her sketchbook with Krushelnytska so that she could peruse the drawings between acts. Salomé had been so distracted, however, that she hadn't had time. Now that her attention was immersed in the labyrinth of the room's objects, however, she had remembered the small, black leather book, and was certain it wasn't there. It was her room, after all. She would know.

She seized Tarsila's hand. "Tell me," she said, "your sketchbook. Where is your sketchbook? You must have returned for it during the show?"

"My sketchbook?"

"Yes! Your book! I'm so sorry to ask you, but did you come back for it?"

"Come back for it? My book?"

"Oh God," Krushelnytska said. "Oh God! Oh God! Stolen! On a ship! How could it be?" Salomé threw up her hands in disbelief.

"Who would steal my sketchbook? Was nothing else taken?" But Tarsila spoke the words only to herself.

"Thief!" Krushelnytska cried. "Thief!"

The detective was at the door a third time, now with two of the ship's uniformed officers. Krushelnytska explained the situation. Before the detective could speak, Krushelnytska preempted him: "Do not tell me the book is still here! You will not be searching my room!"

"But dona Krushelnytska," he said.

"Absolutely not! Search the ship! My God! You will not search my room!"

Krushelnytska slammed the door in the detective's face. She directed the two women who had now arrived to attend to her to search the halls and open rooms for the dog. "Please," she said. "She will not have gotten far. But I do not want her to get to the deck."

She turned to face the mirror. Good God!" she repeated. Each time she said the phrase, it was as though a completely new and baffling thought had occurred to her, as if the mystery continued to provoke more mysterious and more terrifying depths. But then she took a breath and calmed herself. She turned from the mirror. "I'm so sorry," she said. "I'm so, so sorry." And she begged Tarsila to give her leave to take the air.

Krushelnytska hurried to the door. She opened it just a sliver. She peered with one eye. The detective had moved farther down the hallway. There were a few passengers asking questions, and a surly man demanded answers. The detective was very good at keeping them from moving any closer. The two detectives at the other end of the hall gave directions to a group of shipmen on where to search. "Boiler room, lobby, bulkheads, bilge, hold," they said. One by one the men departed, and more arrived to take their place. Salomé charged down the hall and passed the men without a word. Neither did they dare look her in the face.

Inside, Tarsila reclined in the chaise. Her eyes were upon the frescoed ceiling. She contemplated the animals. It was a copy of a famous painting she'd seen. But where? Where had she seen the painting before? The canopy of birds along a river, somewhere in the Amazon of course. She marked the waterfall with her finger, tracing the deep eddies and twists as the river threaded its way through the jungle.

TARSILA MEETS LAIKA AGAIN—
THE PAINTER ACCEDES

AFTER TARSILA LEFT KRUSHELNYTSKA'S SALON, she walked the second-class deck observing late-night revelers, the sleepy, the drunk. She passed down the zigzag stairs and ducked below deck and strayed further down the long hall where the second-class berths were.

She stood on the lower decks watching the files of somnambulant passengers drifting towards their cabins to more sleep and dreams. They carried something of the spirit of Brabant in their steps. Their reveries "took the shape of deep and stalwart feelings of the human heart," as the poet says. The war machine had restored their faithful queen Elsa to her throne. The blackguard Telramund was dead. The Aryan banners flew from the battlements and all was well.

At the end of the hall Tarsila ascended the stairs that led to the bow of the ship, and there she found the tightly packed third-class rooms. Many of the doors were open, and smoke and chatter poured forth into the hallway. The lights were dim, the floors bare. She continued on, ascending another set of stairs, and then arrived on the sun deck, which opened to a view to the ship's horizon, at that moment the night sky. Tarsila considered the moon, a waxing crescent.

From the shadows, a form emerged. It danced towards her, its nails saying *click-clack click-clack*. She felt the small form nuzzle against her leg. She bent down and ran a hand through its shaggy fur. Laika.

For a moment Tarsila counted her options. Fate had tipped its hand when she read the Tarot, and now, here was the proof. The little dog expected her because Tarsila was the Knave who did the Empress's bidding. All of it was written in the cards. Tarsila played the role of emissary. As the aftermath of the theft had played out—a scene in which Salomé departed in such haste, and then the detective had come around again to ask more arbitrary questions about the lost dog and the sketchbook, all of which unfolded aboard the *Vasari* as if on a stage—even Tarsila had noticed that Krushelnytska had begun to mourn the loss of the little dog as if it were known and final.

And so now where was the accomplice, The Fool?

The moon disappeared. The dog scurried off. Tarsila heard the rapping of Laika's nails on the wood. She followed the sound as the dog disappeared into the fog, but then her hand found the railing of a set of stairs, and she followed the sound down, down, down, like falling into vapor.

Then Tarsila was at the lower deck. Laika was there at the bottom of the steps, sitting and waiting. Tarsila followed her below, into the stables, and found the Fool soon enough. From the shadows he greeted Tarsila in a language that sounded German or Spanish but meant nothing to her. He bent down and petted the dog, then stood up and again spoke a few words which she took to be part of his name, "Nathan." He held out his hand and she shook it and smiled.

Tarsila scooped Laika into her arms. She tickled her behind her ears and kissed her. And then Tarsila gave Laika to Nathan. She also handed him her sketchbook.

"Laika," she said. "How curious." Then: "Go, my beloved. Many waters cannot quench love; neither can the floods drown it. Make haste."

Tarsila nodded to Cohen, put her hand on his shoulder, nodded again, then turned. She walked towards the open door of the stables and vanished. Neither saw the other again.

The next day, and the day after that, Tarsila only heard that Krushelnytska shunned visitors and kept to her salon. One midnight, Tarsila spied Krushelnytska walking alone on a promenade. She found Krushelnytska's cabin and slipped the single drawing of Laika she had taken under the door. What would Krushelnytska think? A conspiracy? A delicate gesture? Something maddening? Hopefully she would find some pleasure or comfort in it.

When Tarsila came back on deck, Krushelnytska was still on the promenade. In the brief light, she saw that Krushelnytska was only the perfect Empress. Tarsila left her alone.

* * *

On April 16, 1914, the *Vasari* docked in New York Harbor. Both Tarsila do Amaral and Salomé Amvrosiivka Krushelnytska debarked, each going their separate ways.

Across the Atlantic, in Berlin, the military experimented with new aerial tactics, claiming the aeroplane as the circling dove of peace. Aerial scouts will make war on land impossible, they said, by rendering military strategy impossible. Such is the opinion expressed secretly by great military experts; openly by the people, they said.

The Sun reported "Heavy Frost on Mars": "A heavy late spring frost occurred Wednesday night on Mars in the region north of the propontis, and was still visible at 2 o'clock of the Martian afternoon, according to an announcement from the Lowell Observatory. The frost is extremely heavy. It is parted from the north pole by a blue border, which is undoubtedly water that marks the melting cap, according to the astronomers."

Nathan Cohen had retreated back into the innermost parts of the ship with Laika, and together they lay fast asleep.

TEN

WHAT BECAME OF TARSILA DO AMARAL AND SALOMÉ AMVROSIIVKA KRUSHELNYTSKA

SOME YEARS LATER, after the end of the First World War, Tarsila do Amaral met Salomé Amvrosiivka Krushelnytska a second time, in Milan. The two exchanged pleasantries. Do Amaral had recently shown her work at the Semana de Arte Moderna in Brazil, and had solo exhibitions at the Palace Hotel in Rio de Janeiro and at the Salon Gloria in São Paulo. Krushelnytska congratulated the young painter on her successes, though everything was terribly awkward. Neither woman mentioned the dog or the sketchbook, and after they parted, they never met again.

Krushelnytska returned to her native Lviv in 1934. After the outbreak of the Second World War, she survived both the Luftwaffe shellings in 1939 and then the invasion of the Red Army soon after. Two years after that, the Germans came again, and Lviv remained occupied by the Nazis until 1945, after which Ukrainian and Polish territories were ceded to the Soviets. Krushelnytska spent her remaining years trapped behind the Iron Curtain, giving voice lessons at the Lviv Conservatory.

In 1924, do Amaral returned to Brazil with her lover, the poet Oswald de Adrade and another poet, Blaise Cendrars.

Do Amaral had grown up on a large plantation estate in the town of Capivari, São Paulo. She was the daughter of Jose Estanislau do Amaral Filho and Lydia Dias de Aguiar; and granddaughter of Jose Estanislau do Amaral, nicknamed *o milionário*. In addition to owning twenty-two farms, he built the Teatro São José in São Paulo, the Hotel Internacional in Santos, and the Hotel d'Oeste in Poços de Caldas.

Perhaps as a way of rejecting her family's legacy of slavery, Tarsila do Amaral depicted the working people of Brazil, celebrating them. With inspiration found in the primitivism of painters like Pablo Picasso, Henri Matisse, Paul Gauguin, and Henri Rousseau, do Amaral painted the everyday of her great country. Her paintings were filled with cacti, palms, dense forests, water, gigantic flowers, fruit, and flesh—always flesh. All this in a dreamy landscape of bold, unwavering color. In her return to Brazil, do Amaral wrote: "I feel myself ever more Brazilian. I want to be the painter of my country. How grateful I am for having spent all my childhood on the farm. The memories of these times have become precious for me."

Although the sketchbook was never seen again, there are many paintings that Tarsila did which owe their inspiration to the afternoon she spent with Salomé Amvrosiivka Krushelnytska. The vivid oil painting *Morro da Favela* depicts a shantytown in the tradition of the cubists and surrealists do Amaral studied with in Paris. In the top corner, a woman is hanging laundry. Below, a woman and a man accompany two children to the river in the center of town. Finally, in the lower right-hand corner, another young girl reaches her hand to a small scavenging dog.

Critics who noticed the reoccuring dog in Tarsila's work often remarked that it was a totem representing do Amaral's complicated relationship with her own Brazilian history. The dog represents the mongrels of the favelas, half tame, mostly wild, dangerous; the fila mastiff of the plantations, used to hunt down runaway slaves; the royal *tlalchichi*, guide to Xibalba; *pastor Peruano*, the shepherd; and *campeiro*, killer of feral pigs. And, of course, it was the terrible dog-man Xolotl, god of fire and lightning, who accompanied the sun as it moved through the underworld each night.

For Tarsila, however, the little dog was something altogether different. In her journals, she confided, the fact was that she was haunted by the shaggy dog that appeared in seven different canvases. Each time, the dog was different but the same. In one painting, she faces the child. In another, she turns away. And in still another, she is being led on a leash made from the membrillo vine, with its pink flower tied to her tail. On the day that Tarsila met Laika aboard the *Vasari*, Tarsila had been left with the impression that Laika had no history, or that she was caught between histories. Sometimes Tarsila called her *o viajante do tempo*, the little time traveler.

Tarsila said that she did not actually recollect painting her. Sometimes, after finishing a canvas and leaving it for the night, *viajantinha* would be there in the morning, waiting for her. Other times, she might reconsider a bush or a tree she had painted, dabbing it away with mineral spirits, when, to her surprise, she would find the shape of the dog in the underpainting. Once, she set a trap for her husband suspecting that it was he who was responsible. The trap failed of course, and Behold!

there was the little dog again. Tarsila's journals record both her wonder and fear of the spirit dog. Indeed, she was not a totem at all but a kind of spiritualism.

ELEVEN

A FABLE

VICTORY WAS CERTAIN. Otto von Bismarck had led the Prussian armies to the gates of Paris. The war would soon be over, and Germany would unify as the Second Reich, the Watch on the Rhine.

On September 15, 1870, Prussian forces encircled the capital. Four days later the city was closed. Paris became an island. Sentry balloons were tethered throughout and at the edges of the city, and soldiers were stationed in wicker baskets that hung from them. But reports were inconsistent as they trickled and filtered through official channels and bled out into rumor.

Some said the entire countryside was overrun with Prussian armies, and the fall of Paris would come swiftly and certainly. Others said the siege was the political machinations of the governor, the traitor and coward Louis-Jules Trochu. They said that beyond the city's gates, the Parisian countryside was as naked as a newborn baby. *À poil!* It was a trap to dampen the revolutionary spirit, still alive after the reckoning of the Terror.

"Will we destroy ourselves like animals?

Non!

"Will we succumb under the bourgeoisie?"

Non!

"Break down the gates, storm the countryside, take what belongs to you!"

Liberté, égalité, fraternité!

They said that Otto von Bismarck would shell Paris, and in January he did. The Germans fired twelve thousand rounds into the city over twenty-three nights. By the third week it was madness. Smoke from the fires blanketed the city. The city was a bazaar of wretchedness. Supply shortages were severe. Everything had value. Everything could be bought, sold, or eaten.

And the food! When it could be had, oh it was extraordinary! At the zoo, the two elephants, Castor and Pollux, were killed by firing squad, butchered, and sold on the black market. The trunks went at a premium. Illegal menus were posted in underground dining clubs featuring *consommé, poivrade, flanque, salade.* Unmarked doors were opened by three raps: two short, one long. Inside, the smoke was perfumed with fine tobacco and ambergris, whispers, secrets. The candlelight was a low dream. Soft violins played. There was the elegant clinking of silver on china and the staccato of popping corks on bottles of wine. Where a knife slipped through a juicy rump, stuck in place on tines of silver, a diner sliced apart the recent tragedy of the zoo.

One of the most famous Parisian restaurants, *La Tour D'Argent*, whose chef had up to then performed extraordinary well, found, under the threat of annihilation, depths of inspiration before unimaginable. A ruby-red *glace de trompe* became an event as it laced across sparkling white china. It was a trail of blood that conjured scenes of carnal pleasure.

I've made such sauces, he said. *Béchamel, supreme.* I've whipped *les œuf d'autruche* into immaculate *béarnaise* studded with tarragon picked by the hands of children and slathered on *entrecote d'elefan avec asperges blanches.* I've rubbed tomato paste on knuckle-bones and roasted them to caramel. I've boiled the bones with aromatics and skimmed for a day and a night. Ten liters reduced to a few silvery tablespoons. Now, perhaps, the bones of a water buffalo? Tomorrow, the hippo, whose price they say is still out of reach? What about the ibex or the bear?

Among the delicacies of the extensive zoological menu were *le chameau rôti à l'anglaise, le civet de kangourou, côtes d'œufs rôties sauce poivrade, cuissot de loup en sauce chevreuil, le chat flanqué de rats, et salade de cresson. Garçons* wandered between the diners with whole gnarls of black truffle and caskets of *petits pois.* There were vintages from twenty or thirty years ago. A barrique of Château Beychevelle was emptied in an evening.

No new reports came from beyond the city's walls, and Paris was abuzz with its own goings-on and its own destructions. Letters exchanged hands; industrious children ran notes up and down the streets; mornings were spent scribbling in diaries and journals; and gossip passed between windows, on stoops, down flights of stairs, and across busy streets. Criers shouted through airhorns from the rooftops as if the business of life belonged to everyone, and the news literally flew through the air, written on notes tied to the legs of pigeons that were or sometimes were not lucky to escape the clutches of the ravenous and the mad below. With every significant detail mailed, catalogued, and hastened-on, the city became a babel of storylines whose clamoring routes and passages could only be circumnavigated by arcane magic, spellcasting, necromancy, and Tarot.

One of the surest ways to tell if one is dreaming is to find a clock, a book, a menu, a scrap of language—it can be anything at all. In dreams the writing won't cohere. The lines will blur, or the letters will drift apart. Only in reality does language stick, as if words can't survive the unconscious. Perhaps this is why the people of Paris were so hasty to get everything down on paper—every lie, truth, desire, fantasy, loss, weeping, and penance. The more they recorded, the more they ensured that the nightmare of Paris would resolve and that they weren't in danger of being lost to the terrors of phantasms.

And then, on a frigid, January night, a poet and mathematician of minor celebrity, Gaston Tissandier, climbed the rope of a sentry balloon deep in the heart of Paris, overthrew the man who had fallen asleep on watch, and flew towards the ramparts to the south. He escaped beyond Prussian lines "like an arrow across the mass of clouds." As he sailed over the final ramparts and into the wall of black smoke, the fire of his balloon was like an offering to the god of war, and then it was swallowed and gone.

They said Gaston Tissandier went over the wall and never came back. Or, some say, he did come back eventually, and he told fantastic tales of what he saw beyond the walls of smoke and fire and debris. His travels became the stuff of Baron Munchausen.

In one story, just as the Prussian army had him cornered, Tissandier fired himself from a cannon and rode a cannonball to safety. In another, he was swallowed by a giant sea creature. In still another, he rescued a dog from a mysterious diplomat, a man in furs, who appeared at the gates of Paris with a tale of escaping the Prussians with a dog, Jaune-fille, hidden beneath his coat.

The Jaune-fille variants were immensely popular as they featured the adventures of a down-on-her-luck terrier who, through no fault of her own, becomes the Earth's messenger to the stars. It was a hopeful tale suggesting the magnanimity of the lesser friends of man.

In one story, the pair voyage to the moon to recover Tissandier's lost wits. Launching his airship from the deserts of the Sahara, Tissandier and Jaune-fille travel to the lumber-rooms of the forgotten, "a place wherein is wonderfully stored whatever on our earth we lose: all things whatsoever, lost through time, chance, or our own folly."

In a cave in the Sea of Madness, Tissandier and Jaun-fille discover heaps and troves of vows, unanswered prayers, and lovers' tears and sighs. There are mounds of dead flowers that "formerly distilled sweet savors, and now shed noisome odors." Deeper still, they are lured by a wicked light: one glowing bottle at the far reaches of darkness with a "liquor, soft and thin, which, unless well corked, would from the vase have drained." It is his lost sense.

Tissandier seizes the bottle, but upon exiting the cave, he and his famous dog are captured by the mad moon-king. Just as the king is about execute Tissandier, the queen frees him. He and his dog escape through an underground cavern, which sends them falling back to earth, cushioned on a wave of volcanic air. The two are deposited deep within Vulcan's labyrinthine forge, and there they begin their next adventure.

Paris had been cut off. Its borders were sealed. Yet as the stories of Tissandier's adventures through the heavens continued, so did the Tarot of Paris declaim more peculiar and outlandish tales from beyond the deck. Things that should have been impossible, unimaginable even, wagged regularly on the tongues of the citizens of Paris. The Weird mingled effortlessly into their evening prayers. Yet, these freakish doings, having been appended to their innermost and secret personal mysticisms through the nearly transcendental and transparent channels of the power of suggestion—these surfeits of imagination went mostly unnoticed, excepting by the spellcasters who had developed an eye or a taste for the infernal. It was as if Tissandier had thrown them a rope from the margins with which they might effect an escape. Children were especially susceptible, and more than once a child disappeared up the rope into the dead of night, never to be seen again.

There was heroism in Tissandier's stories, these incalculable ciphers from beyond the stars. The tales suggested lines of flight from the strangling grip of the Prussian-Parisian war machine, what the famous twin poets called "the movement of smooth space, and the movement of people in that space." Tissandier hadn't simply fled. He was a Deserter, a Saboteur: "human, spiritual, and faceless."

On the other hand, it seems equally probable that, having achieved the apex of the night, and the nadir of lost causes in the infinity of space, Tissandier simply threw himself over the railing of his airship. Maybe it is for that reason that his stories continued. He was no longer bodily present to put an end to such unrealistic fantasies. Thanatos is, after all, a death wish, a death drive, and life cannot come from death.

As for the real Gaston Tissandier, he left the Tarot when he escaped to the heavens. Finding himself absent from the deck, as he inevitably did, he no longer carried any relation-ship to its infinitely crossed destinies. He no longer assumed the responsibility of participating in its stories. Thus he shed his karma and wandered freely towards his meaningless and perfect ending.

TWELVE

LAIKA'S WISH—ESCAPE—AN ENDING, OF SORTS

MAY, 1914. "Five hundred thousand war veterans," a corre-
spondent in Servia reported, "each armed to the teeth, each
as ready and willing to die as a frog is ever ready and willing
to jump into water, and each waiting only for the psychological
moment which each and all consider inevitable. This is the nice
little war cloud that is still nursing itself down on the borders of
the Balkans. And this is the nice little war cloud which Servia
says that European diplomacy can never conjure away until it
has either broken out into war and won, or broken out into war
and irretrievably lost forever."

An announcement appearing in European and American newspapers advertised, "For more than two years Mexico
has been in the throes of a great revolution. Railroads have
been destroyed, plantations devastated; mines and ranches
abandoned. Property values have been forced down in many
cases to 10 cents on the dollar of their actual value and in some
cases for even less than this. History repeats itself. The great
opportunity that was presented to the Rothschilds in France,
the East Indian Company in India, our own people at the time
of the Civil War, and other depressed times, NOW presents

itself to you. Never has there been such an opportunity to buy property in Mexico at such depressed prices."

In the Jewish Pale, "the Black Hundreds have again become active, taking advantage of the race hatred roused by the recent 'ritual' trial at Klef. It is hoped by widespread and systematic terrorism to create panic among the Jews which will ultimately result in their wholesale emigration, or, failing that, extinction."

In Bauska, the land was finely dressed in rime and frost.

* * *

It's often said that the Tarot is the journey of The Fool, *Le Mat*. The seventy-eight other cards in the deck are his fates, companions, fears, obstacles, pitfalls, nightmares, and many, many deaths. As the Tarot unfolds, all the forking paths can be written in its outfolding infinities. There are far more permutations of stories written in the Tarot than there are stars in the universe.

There are also tutelary spirits scattered throughout the Tarot. These protectors and guardians are often disguised as animals. The Star empties her flasks into a river where a dolphin swims. A hawk alights on the shoulder of the prince in the Seven of Batons. A shaggy yellow dog nips at The Fool's heels, and together they plunge headlong into destiny.

Sometimes the animal spirits are harbingers of things to come. Sometimes, as in the case of the serpent who coils around the Ten of Staves, they are ambivalent and ambidextrous. The Ten could reference the serpent in the Garden, the staff of Moses, or the *naga*, whose baneful hood shields the Buddha as he meditates, and which is often said to represent fleeting mortality. The tutelars are the sprites who mouth the words of Fate in the myths and symbols that have been appended to them.

The long-eared black wolf, for example, who haunts the margins of The Moon: she is the pathfinder, the wild spirit, a symbol of solitary courage. Her double is the tame dog, who kneels opposite. Yet the black wolf and the tame dog and the dolphin and the hawk and even the shaggy dog—they are all Fate's projections. The Star pours from the amphora, bathing her own discipline. The dolphin is the sign of The Star's wild intelligence. It is one thing to be a symbol. It is another to have the agency of the Wheel, the Chariot, or the Hierophant.

For nine months Laika had been an unseen spirit aboard the *Vasari*. She was expert at keeping to the shadows. Mostly she scavenged the ship's intestines: the boiler rooms, coal forges, engine rooms, and turbines. Late at night she appeared on the promenade, the boat deck, and in the lounges and galleys and dining halls. As she skulked, she discovered the things people left behind and she took them. They were things that could be useful: a scarf, a pamphlet, a rag, a handkerchief. She carried them in her mouth and deposited them at the foot of Nathan Cohen's ladder. When he descended, he picked the thing up, inspected it, and set it in his footlocker until he could find a proper use.

In return for the items she took, Laika deposited small talismans as a sign of fair exchange. Mostly these were abandoned scraps from the workshop and the ship: yarns, a frayed bit of rope or cloth; the wooden curlicues from a bore, beautiful esses of pine, cherry, oak. Sometimes she left a flower that had dropped from a vase—a lily or a rose, or maybe a tuft of laurel. She left her prizes on benches and sills, in front of cabin doors, and on the observation decks. Sometimes the objects were found. More often they were swept away by the crew at the end of the day.

There were a few on the ship who saw her, and they whistled for her, "Little Fairy." Most of the crew had known about Salomé Amvrosiivka Krushelnytska's lost dog and the subsequent appearance of a similar dog that now sometimes accompanied Nathan Cohen. It was an open secret that Nathan's dog made its home below decks, amongst the other animals. They accepted her, like the man, as a good omen. The seamen marshalled all the good spirits of the ocean that they could. If not, the Devil knew how to row. The shaggy dog was a guardian spirit, playful, mischievous, the sign of companionship and adventure. On a dark night when the wind lashed like a whip, and lightning struck freely, she wove invisible threads of *tikkun* throughout the ship.

That May night, as tempests blossomed in the east, squalls that would soon engulf the globe in conflict, the moment had come when Fate would play her weird hand. Laika watched Cohen with his "thick black beard, long tangled hair, and bare legs and feet," from her wooden box beneath the table. He worked over a minute drawing in the small black leatherbound sketchbook beneath a patch of lamplight. "His pants were tawny velvet, but so ragged that they showed his skin in several places—or they were otherwise simply patched." On the other hand, "How dreary to be somebody! How public—like a frog," as the poet says.

On one side of the alcove there was a workbench, with machinery for making small repairs. Above the bench was cargo space, stacked with hay bales.

The noises of the ship were muffled through the heavy wood paneling, a rhythmic *thump-and-turn* as if a thick chain were being swung out and dragged across the floor. Cohen scanned his finger along the drawing and paused. The page was a schematic for the airship: a wooden raft with a tent in the center, and with a ribbed balloon held aloft.

He crossed to one of the closets, checked behind him, opened the door, removed a panel of floorboard, checked again, and then removed a length of rope with a small mechanism attached to the bottom.

Thump-and-turn.

He opened the sketchbook, which was now filled with his plans. A page came loose, and he held it up to the light. A diffused image of the drawing glowed in silhouette. Miniscule schematics lined the edges, and these were connected to the ship with dotted lines.

Cohen bent down and changed part of the apparatus, measured its length, then re-attached it with a steel pin. On the bench was a cylindrical brazier made from the two quarter-hoops of a barrel and forged together with pounded and leveled horseshoes and iron ties. He attached the mechanism, then installed a grate which held it in place, preventing ash from clogging the vents. Satisfied, he wrapped the brazier in a sheet of canvas.

Thump-and-turn.

The dinner bell rang and Laika pricked her ears. She skirted the hardware and tack on the floor and arrived at Cohen's side wagging her tail. Cohen reached down and stroked her muzzle. He rose and took his threadbare coat. He pulled the sheet of silk from the wall and stowed it in the rafters. He replaced the tools. Laika crawled hastily back to the wooden box to await Cohen's return.

Cohen joined a few of the other crew on their way to the dining hall. Passengers, too, were leaving their rooms, ascending from the central D-decks as the last light of the day dropped into the sea. First-class passengers, having already dined, strolled the top deck. They disappeared into halls and salons for the evening's entertainment. The second-class dining room was full. All two hundred passengers were seated in the massive room, which was lively with music and chatter.

The final bell rang, and Cohen joined his shipmates in another dining hall, a sparse room with a long plank table and benches below. Serving platters were piled with fresh bread, biscuits, roast beef with gravy, sweet corn, boiled potatoes, and plum pudding with sweet sauce and fruit, in plain service. When the crew sat, they withdrew forks and napkins from drawers beneath the table. Most had knives of various sizes and shapes that were stashed on their persons. Some sharpened them on the tines of the forks. The port windows were wide open. It was a fine fall evening in May. When they crossed the equator, after midnight, it would be a fine spring evening.

Dinner was over and the moon had risen. Cohen climbed a set of stairs to an observation deck. The black ocean bled into the black night sky. The ship was the center of the universe, a drifting planet with its moon in tow. Cohen stood at the railing. The ship sliced the water in two.

Back in the stables, the crewmen finished the evening chores. Cohen took a bowl from one coat pocket and a bindle from another. Inside the napkin was a share of his dinner. He slipped the bowl into the dark of the alcove where Laika was waiting.

The animals were fed and bedded. The tack was stored. Hatches were secured, windows shut, vents checked and re-checked. The cows brayed. Dogs paced in kennels, shouting at the moon. Turkey, pheasants, parrots, macaws, cockatoos, passerines, and rhea, all squawked and bantered, fluttered in crates and spilled feathers into the dark. Guanaco, llama, and alpaca spit and crowed. Then the lamps were doused and most of the animals became quiet.

Past midnight everyone had retired to their hammocks and cabins. The stables were quiet with the sleeping bulk of animals. Cohen rose and began to take his bed apart. He shut-tled the pieces down the ladder. Laika waited below. She licked his bare foot and hand when he descended.

Within the hour the frame was a secure set of rolled bundles tied with leather. Cohen hauled the bundles through the stables to the staircase that ascended behind the crew quarters. The stairs opened alongside the cargo crane, on the ship's outer bow. There were walls of rigging, rope, and sandbags. The fog had settled. Nobody was afoot. Cohen knew the ship and kept to the shadows.

Cohen returned for the brazier and the balloon. Laika's nails tick-clacked echoes like a code written in pins. Soon the entirety of bundled airship had been brought on deck, and Laika followed the man up the stairs to the cargo deck.

They concealed themselves behind the crane. The crow's nest was in their sightline, but they were camouflaged in the rigging from the masts and the eights of ropes bolted to the deck. Cohen began to assemble the raft. It was quick work. The planks he'd used for the frame of his bed fit together in dovetails, and soon the raft showed its bare ribs. Some of the beams were marked with his scrawls, crisscrossed maps of planets and the articulations of stellar bodies.

Cured staves were laid as planks and lashed with leads and reins. One day he had been asked to throw an empty barrel over the side of the ship but he'd kept it. For weeks he tempered the wood in the steam of the boiler room, then baked the planks flat under the engines. He'd chosen four of the staves for tent poles, and these he'd lathed to perfection. He fitted them into holes in the crossbeams he'd drilled with a bore.

Next came the tent. North, south, east, west: there was a stake for each of the cardinal directions. The fourth of the *sefirot*, *Chesed*, is kindness, mercy, compassion. In fours, perfection. As in the Psalms,

Forever will the world be built with Chesed;
As the heavens, with which You will establish
Your faithfulness.

Cohen fitted panes of canvas around the tent stakes with plow-pin hitches. He secured the poles to the raft with rope knotted from cotton and hemp cord. He laid the roof, reeds and boughs, corn stalks, bamboo, and grass, which he'd collected over many weeks and months as vegetable and timber cargo was loaded on and off the ship. He was careful to leave gaps where the moon could show through. It was a holy *sukkah* that would make its living place among the stars.

Finally, he brought out his prize, what had been the lining of his mattress. The balloon's canopy was a magnificent dreamcoat of patterns and color. It was a patchwork of discarded items he had collected from passengers who were known for buying entire traveling kits before they departed and then chunking them when their vacations were over. There were spotted, checkered, and plain white cotton handkerchiefs. A rainbow of silk ties, ascots, neckerchiefs, and drapes. There were paisley, green cotton linen, green flax linen, and burgundy and blue velvet trousers. There were fancy dresses, men's coats, and children's britches. Once someone left behind a green, rabbit-fur coat. Each item had been carefully plucked apart, seam by seam, unfolded, measured, cut, and then quilted back together. The heavy homespun stitching that zigzagged through the pastiche of material was "like a tattoo of ancient hieroglyphics, perhaps a complete theory of the heavens and the earth, or a mystical treatise on the art of attaining truth," as the poet says. The balloon was reinforced with bamboo spars, which drew the fabric into a collapsed sphere. The mouth was fitted with another of the barrel's steel hoops. He hefted the balloon towards one of the ship's steam vents and fitted on the metal ring.

Laika watched and for a moment nothing happened. Then, as air vented from the galleys below was piped into the balloon, the cloth began to ripple and rise. It snaked along the deck in rapid, lively breaths, and then it settled into a steady inflation, a long draw of fevered breath as it unfurled into the night. Cohen lashed the balloon's ropes and drew the brazier from out of the shadows.

Until moments ago, they had been invisible. But now that the balloon was airborne and the motor was set to work, humming and belching hot air, and keeping the balloon aloft, the airship entered the world.

Laika boarded and circled the deck. She inspected the riggings, the tent, and the tiny store of provisions stashed in a wooden trunk. The airship was the aggregation of thousands of collected fragments, and many months of wanderings aboard the *Vasari*, all caught within the steamship's long orbit between New York and Brazil. To imagine a coherence of time in that nebulous limbo would have been remarkable. Yet the airship was a single thought: perfect and untouchable.

And then there was no more time. The night watch would soon arrive. Cohen unfastened the hitches that held the ship in place. Laika paced the deck of the raft. She barked twice, sounding her barbaric yawp, and wagged her tail. The airship went aloft. It lurched unsteadily in a flare of passion, then resolved into the calm language of a long voyage, steadfast and certain, unconcealed and defenseless.

Amongst the constellations and galaxies of possibilities in the Tarot, occasionally The Fool is separated from his companion. Indeed, there are endings in the Tarot, and they are often marvelous and exceptional.

In one draw, The Fool and his companion come to the Tarot's outer limits. There are signs: The Wheel of Fortune, The Hanged Man, The Nameless Arcanum, The Tower, The Star, Judgment, The World. This is the edge of the knowable. Further on are the depths of chaos, where stories emerge and tangle, unspool and perish.

The dog dances merrily at The Fool's feet. The Fool sets his staff down and unties the bindle. Both he and the dog find a soft spot to sit in the thick green grass at the ledge. They have come many miles together, although they've only just met. There is the quality of always to everything that goes before and after.

Suddenly, amongst the lightning and fire at the Universe's outer edges, a small craft appears. They did not know they had been waiting for it, but when the boat appears neither is surprised.

There is only enough space for one of them. There are only a few such wormholes in the universe of Tarot, and there is no guarantee that they will even be played. They are fleeting moments of vast (un)doing. At this juncture, it's possible that either The Fool or his companion, never both, might be ripped? loosed? set free? birthed free? from the yoke of narration.

The Fool removes a candle from his backpack and lights it. He brings the light to his face like a blessing. He lights incense and waves it in the four directions of His name. At the crossroads of the night, at the edge of the sky where night joins morning, he who has no birth and yet always exists, who is always becoming yet never is—The Fool makes a simple gesture for peace.

> If some aspire to the realms above the moon,
> then he has chosen to dwell beneath it,
> and so shoulder that planet's shadow.

Earth touches sky. Night touches morning. The little dog boards the craft and sails into the night. The fissure closes. In the morning, the deck is reshuffled and played again.

THIRTEEN

CODA

ON THE MORNING OF AUGUST 15, 1942, merchant marine officer Milton Fernandes da Silva woke to the crash of lightning. He tried to turn on his light but found there was no electricity. He put his uniform on over his pajamas, climbed the stairs, then heard the commander shouting to another soldier ahead. "What was that, Benedito?"

"We have been torpedoed sir!"

Ponham os coletes salva-vidas e corram às baleeiras! said the commander: Put on your lifejackets and run to the lifeboats!

Da Silva made his way past the first two *baleeiras* when he felt the second and third torpedoes strike. He descended the balustrades until he reached the keel, found the ship to be nearly horizontal, and jumped into the water where he was pulled under by the suction of the sinking ship. Miraculously, he was able to return to the surface and swam for a piece of awning attached to part of the cargo hold. Once he'd recovered, da Silva was able to rescue three more people he saw floating in the debris in the water, bringing them alongside his raft.

In the next few hours, da Silva salvaged what he could find, and from wherever he could find it. Meanwhile, the *Araraquara* sank in a nightmare of fire and death. "Strokes fell with a measured beat, and a certain rattling of iron and chains and the furious din of water," as they say.

The men stayed afloat for seven days before they began to succumb to hallucinations and dehydration. One man kept asking for food, saying that he'd heard the bell rung for coffee. The others tried to calm him down, but suddenly the man attacked, then jumped into the water and swam away towards the open ocean. Another man fell into a fit, and he too threw himself into the water, and by floating on his back, he used an oar to row himself away.

After spending another three days at sea, da Silva and the last remaining man, the ship's oiler, spotted the lights of Aracaju on the horizon. They were carried by the ebb tide of the Continguiba River, and landed on the outer beaches of Estancia. Nearby, in the low water, face down, lay the man who had rowed away. His forehead touched sand that was sometimes, between each wave, above the sea, as the poet says. The two men laid down and slept.

In the morning they harvested green coconuts, drinking the water and eating the pulp. Da Silva retrieved whatever else might prove useful: two knives, two strands of rope, and empty bottles that he hoped to fill with fresh water. He found one that was corked and contained a letter of some kind. He stashed the bottle in an inside coat pocket. He also collected the personal effects of two more men he found drowned on the beach and stowed them carefully away.

Da Silva and the oiler walked two-and-a-half leagues before coming upon the jungle finca of Luiz Gonzaga de Liveira. They passed through acres of coffee beans and cacao until they found a cabin from which black smoke was rising. They smelled the meat searing in the smoke that drifted their famished way.

At the cabin they found Gonzaga de Liveira, who, after having spent the afternoon hunting, was dressing a thatch of pheasants amid a blanket of bloodied palm fronds. He sat the men down and offered them a plate of pheasants he had just removed from a spit, a bottle of red wine, and bade the two men eat and drink before they told him their story.

The next day Liveira took them by canoe to San Cristóvão. They arrived at nine a.m. and were greeted by the mayor of the town. Like Liveira, the mayor invited them to his home, obliging them to eat a small meal, then took them on to the Hotel Marozzi to be treated by the town doctor. They remained there for the next two weeks.

During those days, other rescuees from the *Araraquara* appeared: José Pedro da Costa, a barber, who saved himself by floating on a piece of board; Mauricio Ferreira Vital, a steward, who was picked up by a fishing boat; Eunice Balman, Jose Rufino dos Santos, José Coirreia dos Santos, Francisco José dos Santos, all sailors; and José Alves de Mola, a stoker and fireman. Da Silva showed the men the belongings he'd found. Upon opening the corked bottle, da Silva discovered what appeared to be the schematics for a hot air balloon, set adrift amidst a sea of bizarre script that neither he nor the other men could decipher.

A week later, da Silva turned over the bottle and other collected artifacts and possessions to Brazilian authorities when he made his deposition.

Of the 142 people aboard the merchant ship *Araraquara*, only eleven survived. The wreck of the ship marked the second of seven ships sunk in the bloody weeks of August, when the infamous U-507, a Nazi U-boat under the command of Fregattenkapitän Harro Schacht, patrolled the Brazilian coast. Sailing during what was called *zweite glückliche Zeit*, the second happy time, or The American Shooting Season, Schacht attacked all boats he came across, without first ascertaining nationality.

The last to be sunk was the *Jacyra*, with six people aboard and carrying a cargo of cacao, coconuts, bananas, and piaçaba, along with boxes of empty bottles and a dismantled truck. The *Jacyra* was sunk by four scuttling charges, and its entire crew escaped on a life raft, landing at Serra Grande beach. On September 15, Schacht was recalled by German patrol to aid in the rescue of fifteen hundred Italian prisoners aboard the RMS *Laconia*, off of the coast of West Africa. When the U-boat was attacked by US fighter planes, Schacht abandoned the rescue mission, diving into the deep waters of the Atlantic and disappearing. Later, and as a direct result of the incident, Germany banned all U-boats from aiding in rescue operations.

On August 23, 1942, only two days after the eleven survivors of the *Araraquara* landed at Estancia, the *New York Times* reprinted Brazil's declaration of war on Germany, citing the following:

> Without consideration for [the] peaceful attitude of
> Brazil and under the pretext of a need to make to-
> tal war against a great American nation, Germany
> attacked and sank without previous warning vari-
> ous Brazilian merchant units which were engaged
> in commercial navigation…Despite the simplest

principles of humanity, five vessels, the *Baependy*, *Annibal Benevolo*, *Arara*, *Araraquara* and *Itagiba*, were attacked on the Brazilian coast while traveling in coastal commerce...There is no way to deny that Germany and Italy practiced war acts against Brazil, creating a belligerent situation that we are forced to recognize in defense of our dignity and sovereignty.

Thus it was that Brazil entered into the Second World War.

Fifty years after the end of World War II, the Museu da Força Expedicionária Brasileira, in Rio de Janeiro, hosted a memorial honoring the role of Brazil's Expeditionary Force: the three divisions of infantry, liaison flight, and fighter squadrons who fought from September 1944 to May 1945. For the semicentennial, many new items from the museum's archives were catalogued and put on display. Among the personal artifacts were a handmade camera made of salvaged electrical parts; a small blade hidden in a business card case; a tiny coffin, small enough to fit in the palm of one's hand, and sent to those who collaborated with the Axis; boots made from the Toquilla palm and sent to the Eastern Front; a packet of cigarettes that had been dropped over occupied Netherlands, which carried the message, Nederland zal herrijzen! (The Netherlands will rise again!); sets of coins in different currencies given to agents parachuting into enemy territories; examples of forged Reichskleiderkarte (books of ration stamps); patches with the Expeditionary Force's motto,

Senta a Púa! (Go get 'em!); and a large collection of photos and letters from Brazilian troops.

One letter, from Major General João Baptista Mascarenhas de Morais, describes the first five thousand BEF soldiers, the sixth RCT, who sailed aboard the USS *General Mann*, and arrived in Italy on July 16. The disembarked troops landed without weapons, and, since there was no arrangement for barracks, they slept on the docks.

Also among the artifacts was a small glass bottle, next to which was a hand-drawn schematic for a hot-air balloon in a haze of black smoke. On closer inspection, the smoke turned out to be a fog of writing and drawings. The note and the bottle were found, read the information tag, by Milton Fernandes Da Silva, of the Brazilian merchant ship *Araraquara*, which was torpedoed off the coast of Brazil between Salvador and Aracaju. They belonged to a sailor whose whereabouts and status were unknown, it said: Descrevendo os planos para um navio de ar em uma língua estrangeira…talvez um sinal de afeição…transportado por um dos marinheiros perdidos.

At the bottom of the note were a few lines of Cyrillic script. Though the schematics were annotated in Russian, and though none of the men aboard the *Araraquara* were known to speak Russian or any other Slavic language, apparently there was no reason why such an object would not be in a sailor's possession. Therefore, it aroused little comment, other than to become a single line in an exemplary list of personal property: combat pack, dog tags, belt buckle, poncho, class ring, cartridge belt, deck of playing cards, first aid pouch, canteen, entrenching shovel, etc. There were photographs and a diary, and the schematics were included as one of the pages of personal artifacts. The men were sailors. They had travelled the world. And Brazil was a cosmopolitan metropolis where more than one hundred and fifty different languages were spoken. An indecipherable page with Russian script was maybe an amusement.

A year after the Museu celebrated its semi-centennial, however, the great-grandniece of one of the first Jewish settlers in Argentina visited the museum. She saw the note and could read some of the Russian. She also noticed a very faded signature at the bottom: Moisésville. The woman called for a docent, who, misunderstanding the woman's request, told her that Moisés was not the person who drew the map. When the woman explained that Moisésville was actually a Jewish settlement in Argentina, the docent called an archivist, and together they examined the drawing.

They found that the schematics for the airship had been drawn over a letter, which itself had been palimpsestically eroded, so that only the briefest fragments could still be read. The letter was a history of histories, one opening onto the next in the flat plain of a page of paper.

Moisésville was the location attached to the original note. Other remnants included the words коровы, саранча, счастливые, and семейные (cows, locusts, happy, and family); and the partial name *Froim Zal*—and the word *Bauska*. None of the three could work out the meaning of the latter. They agreed that the drawing may have once belonged to someone associated with Moisésville, so the archivist agreed to forward the letter on to Museu Judaico in Buenos Aires.

Not until another ten years later, however, was the Cyrillic script finally translated. It was found by an old dusty sub-librarian who was doing research in the Museu Judaico's archives. Having some familiarity with what should and should not have been in the archive, the note, along with the letter from the Museu da Força Expedicionária Brasileira, caught his attention.

In a catalog entry he created for the schematic, he wrote that there had been a simple *mix up*. Although the schematic and the bottle had been discovered with the wreck of the *Araraquara*, the two events were purely coincidental. A *lucky draw*, he said. The bottle must have already been floating in the water when it was mixed in with the wreckage. In fact, the note was much odder than any of that.

Indeed, in one section of the map there were a few lines that discussed Moisésville, which was a kibbutz near Santa Fe, in Argentina. It mostly recorded numbers and kinds of animals, payments, and the weather. The librarian noted that the lines were probably from the diary page's original author, who at one time was a resident there.

Other phrases indicated a general plan for travel, and some language about the moon. There were calculations for wind speeds and currents, though, taken as a whole, the librarian concluded the math was either a fragment from another more complete thought, which had been among the diary's other pages, or, more than likely, the letter was nonsense.

Near the bottom of the schematic, however, were a few hazy lines written in pencil, which the librarian translated very clearly: "I have landed safely on the moon," it said. "Sometimes you may look up and find me there." Below were the words "Laika" and "SS *Wandering Jew*." The librarian wrote out the lines, but made no comment. Then he catalogued his findings and restored the note—along with other fragments in the paper box he had been working on—to the museum's archives.

A NOTE ON SOURCES

Source texts range widely and include the journals of Christoph Arnold, 1674; Anthony Armoux' *The European War: September 1915–March 1916*: Ritter & Company: Boston, Mass., 1917; "Royal Armstead: An Extraordinary History and Mystery" in The Australian Journal, September, 1873; Amaral Aracy's *Tarsila Cronista*, Edusp: 2001; Alejandro Jodorowsky and Marie Costa, *Way of the Tarot*: Destiny Books: 2009; Gershom Scholem's *Kabbalah*: Meridian: New York, 1978; Haim Avni's *Argentina and the Jews*: University of Alabama Press, 1991; and M. F. Maury's *The Amazon and The Atlantic Slopes of South America*, 1853. Quoted newspaper articles were sourced on the Library of Congress' Chronicling America newspaper database, an amazing resource for which I am eternally grateful. Although there is a Nathan Cohen who died at a sanitarium in Green Farms, Connecticut, and was buried at Mount Richmond Cemetery on Staten Island, New York, the Nathan Cohen that appears in this book is only a specter.

ACKNOWLEDGMENTS

Thank you to the faculty in the English Department at the University of Utah, especially Paisley Rekdal, Lance Olsen, Kathryn Stockton, Scott Black, and Jeffrey McCarthy, who read and commented and encouraged and helped make this book possible. Thank you to the Steffenson-Cannon Foundation for their fellowship support, and for their invaluable gift of time. Thanks to Brenda Tipps for your thoughtful comments. Thanks to Emily and Z for being. Thanks to my comrades here in Salt Lake—Dale Enggass, Molly Gaudry, and 'Ilaheva Tua'one. I raise so many glasses to you and your futures. Thanks to FC2, a dream come true. And thanks to you, the reader.